THE UNKNOWN

A COVID-19 CHARITY ANTHOLOGY

The Unknown: A COVID-19 Charity Anthology

For rights, bulk publishing, and other publication information or to report errors, send letter to:
Publisher – Twisted Souls Press
PO Box 569
Roy, Utah 84067

Cover by Sabrina RG Raven.

TABLE OF CONTENTS

THE CHARITY OF CHOICE

The Life On Your Terms Project

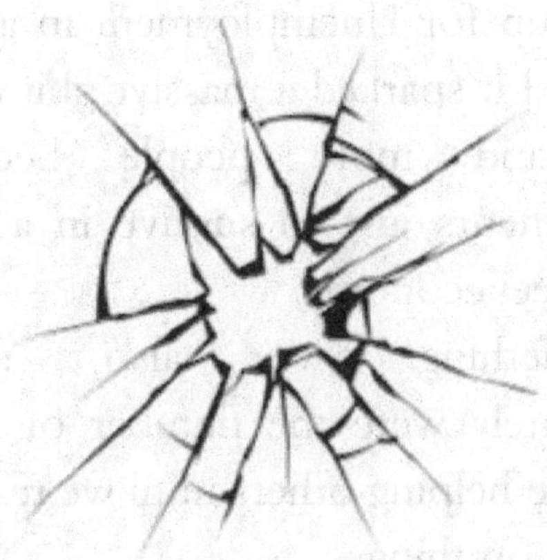

The Life On Your Terms Project was originally created to be a transitional support system for artists. From musicians to writers and everything in between.

It wasn't long after the idea was thought and things were built out to really get it going, when the Coronavirus struck.

The idea behind the charity is to help people wanting to do what they love for a living but being stuck living life on someone else's terms because we all 'gotta pay the bills'.

When the virus hit, and really took hold, we almost immediately saw exactly where things stood when you live life on other people's terms. Millions of people signing up for Unemployment in a single week and it sparked a massive shit toward more and more people becoming entrepreneurs just to survive in a failing 'employee' economy.

Something we also noticed immediately were the number of people that were helping others until we really got a handle on things.

They were out there, which is great, but the way things are set up, it really isn't enough to keep going.

We've read the horror stories and watched all the movies. We know what happens with people when the resources to be able to take care of ourselves, let alone others, runs out.

That is when things really get scary. So, The Life On Your Terms Project shifted gears. We don't want to see horror stories becoming our reality and we firmly believe that the only way to mitigate the really bad stuff from happening is to not just keep those people helping other people, but also encouraging others do the same.

And keep doing it.

We haven't reached the point of no return, yet. We are still at the point that with enough effort and support, we can help other people. Sure, we could give to some giant organization that can distribute a lot more quickly and easily than we can, but they also have their limits.

We explored our limits to see what we could do reach the most people and be the most effective, and accomplish our goal of not just helping others, because we are always all about that, but encouraging others to do whatever they can.

That is the purpose of this anthology. To encourage the spread of helpfulness to others and avoid the spread of self-preservation. When we reach the point that everyone is just out to save themselves, that is when things get ugly.

So, here is our plan. This sales of this anthology will be used to buy gift cards in small increments ($20-$50) from different places. Amazon, Hobby Lobby, Gas stations, and grocery stores.

We already have a long list of people that are going out of their way to help other people, by doing things like making face masks and hand sanitizer all the way up to doing weekly grocery runs for their neighbors in order to prevent them falling ill. They are running out of the resources to keep doing it.

Those things need to keep happening so that is the first line we intend to provide assistance to. It won't be much, at first, but it should be enough to get them the materials they need to keep going.

The second line, will be setting up a web space where people can show up and get creative ideas for ways to help people. Once they have decided on the what, they can reach out to us and we can help them work out the how, be it with getting them items they need via material donations all the way up to gift cards.

We have to work together on working together. That is what is ultimately going to keep the fictional stories you are about to read from becoming the reality.

Thank you from the bottom of our hearts for your contribution to keeping kindness and helpfulness to others going!

The Life On Your Terms Project.

Twisted Souls Press.

Every Author that contributed to this anthology.

Anyone and everyone we are able to reach through sales of this anthology.

And the future generations that will be able to look back on these times and be grateful that these stories stayed works of fiction.

FOREWORD

HORROR FICTION: A VACCINE AGAINST FEAR

Josh Schlossberg
JoshsWorstNightmare.com

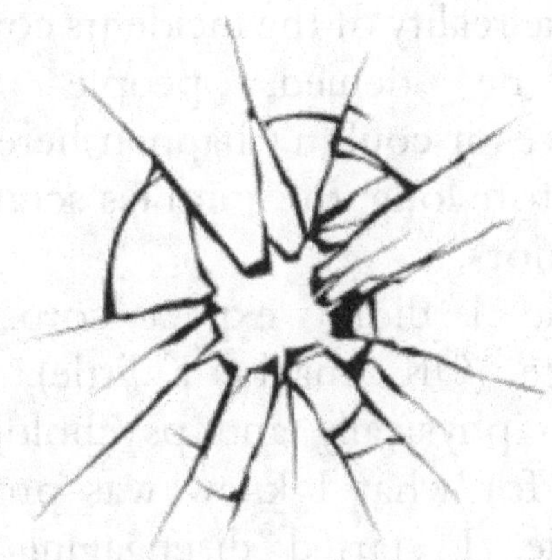

If the COVID-19 pandemic revealed anything about humanity, it's that folks haven't been reading enough horror fiction.

I've been researching/writing/worrying/warning about disease outbreaks in my fiction for over a decade, tracing back to the 2009 H1N1 pandemic. So, in January, while the world was distracted with who was saying what mean words to whom on social media, I was paying close attention to the outbreak of a new respiratory ailment in Wuhan, China.

Having read countless zombie novels, I recognized the plot line: A handful of cases on the other side of the world. Initial reports suppressed or dismissed.

When the reality of the incidents could no longer be denied, people telling themselves it couldn't happen here. And then, before long, the zombies scratching at our doors.

While I didn't expect corpses to reanimate (OK, maybe a little), I did begin to physically and psychologically prepare for what I knew was probably inevitable. I started disengaging from public social events while stocking up on food and other household products, and quietly suggested others do the same (nearly all of whom thought I was crazy).

The result was that, come mid-March, when people were finally starting to wake up to the situation and began freaking out, my anxiety had already peaked and was on the downslope. What that meant was I wasn't further feeding the collective fear by emotional venting, spreading inaccurate (or out of context) information, or prognosticating doom. And speaking of feeding, since I had already procured my necessities during a time of overabundance, I didn't need to do any last-minute panic shopping and add stress to the supply chain.

I apologize if it seems like I'm trying to toot my own horn or point fingers here. I'm really not. I'm just documenting how, if more people had been paying closer attention to horror fiction, there would've been enough toilet paper to go around.

Of course, while horror can certainly warn us about calamities such as disease outbreaks, its much greater benefit is how it can help prevent a lot of needless panic, which is more dangerous than any pandemic.

In other words, reading horror fiction is like a vaccine, inoculating us with a harmless germ of terror to build up our immunity for when the shit really hits the fan.

The COVID-19 pandemic is but one example of multitudes, as we all know life is full of rays of sunlight as well dark twists and turns we'd best prepare ourselves for. This isn't to say we let the shadow consume us by, say, watching *Faces of Death* while drinking wine from the skulls of our enemies. But neither can we afford to pretend it doesn't exist.

To the contrary, people's largely unhelpful and often hysterical reactions to the outbreak prove that the world could benefit from more people building up their tolerance to fear. And it just so happens this anthology is one of the best tools at our disposal to help us get there.

THE UNKNOWN

Christy Mann

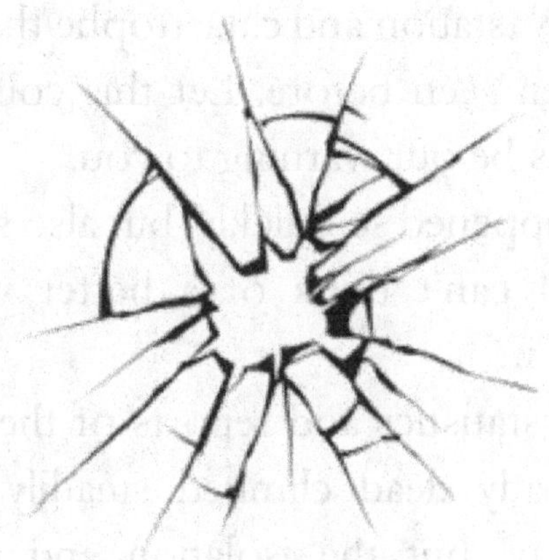

There is a killer among us. It isn't a virus, a disease, or even a sneaky individual on an unhealthy spree. It isn't a natural disaster, mass shootings, or even nuclear war. It's destroying more than we have ever seen before and no one knows how to stop it.

Very few people are able to see it, fewer still recognize it for what it is. Those that do and speak up about it are shut down immediately. Not just by officials, but the people closest to them too. No one wants to talk about it.

No one knows where it came from, and no one can determine where it will go from here. All we know is that it came through, almost out of nowhere, and left more devastation and catastrophe than had ever been seen before. Let this collection of stories be our warning to you.

It happened so quickly, but also so very slowly. I can't think of a better way to describe it.

The statistics and reports of the dying and already dead climbed steadily every single day, but the isolation and forced separation made the days drag together and seem to never end.

Routines no longer exist to the point that only the definition of what one is remains. We no longer venture out so even the words day and night are just...words. We were so worried about becoming ill that our regard and concern for the others waned.

In the early days, we tried. Technology was advanced enough that we were able to connect with people all over the world. We kept in touch, and checked in on the people we knew all the time.

But the day eventually came for everyone that the words that once comforted did nothing but leave us feeling more and more like strangers.

Then the disruptors, as we began to call them, hijacked our communications and bombarded us with horrible images and stories about the dead or dying. Or, about trampling on people's rights.

We called it fear mongering no matter what it was and chose to look the other way. Eventually, we just stopped communicating. We should not have done that.

I was 44 when all of this started. I stopped counting when I think I turned 55. I couldn't begin to tell you how long ago that was now.

I'm old, and very tired now. I don't know who else has made it this long. I hope it is many, but no one has knocked on my door for an eternity. I hope, yes still after all this time, hope that the end of this comes sometime soon for them. It is coming soon, but not soon enough, for me.

There is nothing, and I mean absolutely nothing, worse than just waiting for the unknown to reveal itself.

I'm going to go lay down now. Rest until I either can't rest any more, or...

THE RESEARCHER

Archie Kregear
Author of *Mountain Gods*

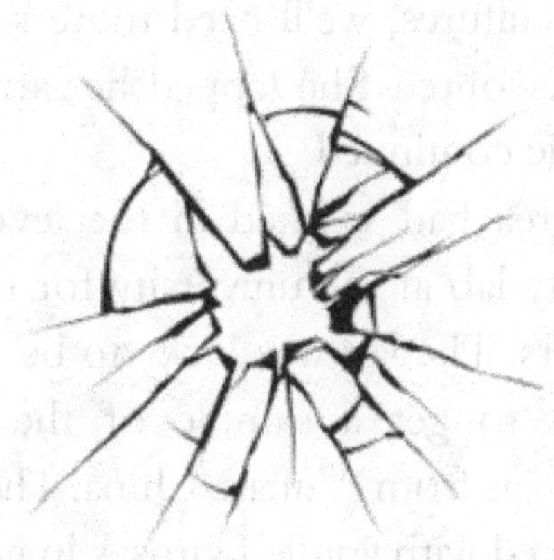

The rock music of Greta Van Fleet helped Dr. Andrea Kua to relax as she took samples of her latest experiment to the scanning electron microscope. The music cut off, and a beep notified her of an incoming message. She tapped the screen attached to the back of her arm, and a note from the director of the lab appeared on the inside of her bio containment helmet.

'Heads up, folks. China is quarantining a larger area. They're becoming more concerned about this new coronavirus.'

What are you, little guy? What are you made of? Andrea asked herself while looking into the sample the lab received yesterday. If I can't replicate this virus on the cell cultures, we'll need more samples from the source. She tapped her arm, and the music continued.

Andrea had worked in the level-four bio-safety lab at the university for the last four years. The lab was lucky to be one of the first to get a sample of the novel coronavirus from Wuhan, China. The team she worked with studied viruses in general. They were especially eager to study this virus spreading in China so they could share their research with labs working on therapeutics and a vaccine. The news from China in this the second week of January was that this new viral pathogen was highly contagious and virulent. Andrea's gut told her that there was no time to waste.

The tissue cultures Andrea grew were like her garden. She gave the cells the nutrients they needed to grow and reproduce, and then harvested a few bits to put under the microscopes. It was slow, tedious work at best. Being encumbered by a positive-pressure suit didn't make anything easy.

Yet she felt completely safe inside the suit required to protect herself from the pathogens she worked with while doing the research she loved.

It was almost five by the time she started the process of leaving the lab. Shutting down equipment, disinfecting and taking the suit off, then taking a shower and getting dressed took nearly an hour. As she was drying off, her phone rumbled like a passing freight train as it vibrated on a shelf inside the old metal locker.

She hung the towel over the locker door and picked up her phone. Kyle had sent a message, asking her to meet him for dinner at the Ethiopian restaurant they liked. Standing naked in the cramped dressing area, she texted Kyle back. 'I'll be there in 45 depending on how soon I can get an Uber.'

Having ancestors of both Chinese and Mediterranean descent, she lacked the Oriental eyes but inherited a lithe, thin frame and straight hair, which she kept long enough to wear in a ponytail. Tonight for dinner, she parted her hair in the middle and let it hang loose.

Andrea met Kyle at a Halloween party in 2018. He came dressed as Sheriff Woody and Andrea went as a butterfly. He was hooked the moment he saw her. Kyle was cute and smart, and as she got to know him she found him to be very respectful. He had an MBA and worked in finance for a local software firm. After fifteen months together she knew he loved her, or at least was in love with the relationship. What more could a thirty-year-old woman want?

Going out to dinner with Kyle's coworker Sean and his wife Linda was something they did at least once a week. Thus Andrea always wore something to work in the morning that she could wear out on the town in the evening.

She found Kyle, Sean, and Linda at the restaurant bar, already enjoying a drink.

'I ordered you a glass of Chardonnay,' Kyle said, holding out a wine glass.

Andrea accepted it with a kiss. Then she hugged Linda and Sean. She enjoyed the people Kyle brought into her life, and he enjoyed spending time with her friends. Life in the city was good.

On Sunday, the nineteenth of January, Andrea and Kyle had dinner with her parents, who owned a property management business. Last summer, when they decided to move in together, her father had found a suitable apartment for Kyle and her near the university.

During dinner, Andrea's dad asked her, 'What do you know about this virus in China?'

Andrea replied, 'I know everything published so far.'

'Should we be worried about it?' asked Andrea's mother.

'This virus is serious. There is no immunity to the virus, no treatment, or vaccine. I'm concerned about the data we receive from China; the reports are conflicting. Right now make sure you have enough food stored for a month, which you should always have anyway.'

'We don't have a month's worth of food in our apartment,' said Kyle. 'Where would we put it?'

'I'll go shopping this week and get some dry staples. They won't take a lot of space,' said Andrea.

Andrea's mom began to list everything she had stored for an emergency. Andrea made a mental list of what they would need and hoped this coronavirus would not lead to a pandemic.

That week Henry Williams, the director of the lab where Andrea worked, asked everyone to increase their work hours. There were no cases of the new virus in the United States, but the news from China kept getting worse. Andrea altered her life a little by going to work earlier in the mornings and on weekends. That way, she still had time with Kyle and their friends in the evenings.

Over the next few weeks, her lab and other labs around the world confirmed the sequence of the RNA containing the genetic code for the virus. They knew the proteins making up the capsule, the spikes, and the matrix of the envelope. They documented the method of how the virus entered cells to reproduce. Daily, Andrea and others of her team would make scanning electron micrograph images of the virus to determine its structure.

In the first week of February Andrea sent a document to Director Williams, summarizing the details they had learned thus far. In it, she wrote, 'The novel Coronavirus has some RNA sequences similar to SARS of 2003 and primarily affects the respiratory organs. This suggests the name Severe Acute Respiratory Syndrome Coronavirus 2 (SARS-CoV-2).'

The director added his edits and forwarded the document to the broader scientific community worldwide. On February twelfth, Director Williams mentioned to Andrea that the International Committee on Taxonomy of Viruses had taken her suggestion, that SARS-CoV-2 became the name of the virus, and the disease it causes is COVID-19. It was like the second ship in the Star Trek series having the name NCC-1701 B. Coming up with the name was too obvious to give credit to someone.

Andrea began experimenting on ways to attack and neutralize SARS-CoV-2 during the infectious stage and examining paths to produce a vaccine. As more news started to arrive from South Korea, Iran, and Italy, she became a one-topic conversationalist when out with friends, commenting only on the epidemic. At night she dreamt about the virus and discovering a molecule that could counter its deadly march through humanity.

At the end of February, over dinner at an English pub, the coronavirus entered the conversation. Kyle said, 'I think you're obsessed with COVID-19. Are you sure it hasn't infected your brain?' He tapped on the side of her head and chuckled.

Andrea batted Kyle's hand away, and for the first time in their relationship she was sharp with him. 'This is the worst pathogen in years. I'm frightened by what I know.'

'How many people are infected in the U.S.?' asked Sean.

'Three new confirmations today,' replied Andrea. 'Worldwide, there are eighty-five- thousand with this virus.'

'That's less than one infected person in every hundred-million Americans,' Linda observed.

'There are fewer people infected than are at a Wolverine home football game,' added Kyle. 'It's all you think about lately.'

'I want to stop this virus before it kills more people. Italy and Iran are now hot spots. This is what I studied my ass off for eight years to do.'

'Tell me again what your degree is in,' Linda requested.

'I have a doctorate in Microbiology and Immunology. The lab where I work specializes in molecular pathogens like viruses.'

'Okay,' Kyle said, holding up his hands in a surrender pose. 'You know what you're talking about.'

'Say the words, Kyle,' said Sean.

'What words?' Kyle asked with a dumbfounded look.

'He doesn't have to apologize,' Andrea said. 'What I want everyone to know is that I think this virus has the potential to be devastating.'

Sean leaned in to ask, 'So, what's your motivation for stopping COVID-19? Do you have a hero complex and want to save the world? Do you think that you'll get rich from a vaccine? Or do you want to be famous?'

'I-I never thought…'

Kyle interrupted, 'What I know is that Andrea is the smartest, prettiest, sexiest, and most together person I have ever known. She will solve this because she can.'

'I'll drink to that,' said Sean. 'Cheers!'

Andrea felt a little embarrassed by the attention, but Kyle's words dissolved her indignation. She took a big sip from her wine glass.

On Sunday, the eighth of March, while having dinner at her parents, Andrea said, 'Stay home this week, maybe the next two weeks. Then we'll see how the virus is spreading in the U.S.'

Kyle replied, 'You're too close to the bad news. I'm sure it's affecting you. I can't stay home this week.'

Andrea's mom said, 'We can't just up and abandon our business.'

'Don't go out,' Andrea implored. 'Every contact with a person or with anything a person has touched is a chance to become infected.'

Her father spoke up, 'We'll be more careful about meeting clients and wash our hands more often. We haven't changed our lives because of anything in the past, and I'm not going to change now.'

Andrea wondered if she was paranoid and overreacting. The epidemiologist she worked with was one of the few people she knew who agreed with her assessment of the danger. The next morning, she packed a bag of clothes and the things she would need for two weeks. She left a note for Kyle, telling him that she was afraid of infecting him and that he should remain isolated until she said it was safe. She signed, 'I love you.'

That afternoon, Andrea received a text. 'Is Italian good for dinner?'

Andrea sighed and thought for a moment before composing a reply. 'I'm going to focus on work for a while. Please be safe.'

Andrea continued to worry about her parents and Kyle. What could she say to get them to isolate themselves? She was frustrated to have the people closest to her refuse to heed her warning. Her only hope of saving them came down to developing a vaccine. She did as much as she could while awake, and slept on a cot in an empty office at night.

A text came from Kyle on Wednesday evening, 'The NBA is suspending the season because a player tested positive for the virus. You're right. It's spreading.'

Andrea called her mother. 'How are you?'

'We're fine. Your father and I were just discussing the virus. We agreed to go out only for emergencies. How are you?'

Andrea felt some relief, as she would not need to plead with her parents to stay home. 'I'm fine. I'm staying at the lab for a while.'

'You're not at home?'

I'm in a locked-up building on campus,' Andrea responded. Knowing her mother's fears for her physical safety, Andrea added, 'The building has a security guard.'

'How will the security guard protect you from the virus?'

'I'll tell him to shoot the virus on sight,' said Andrea.

Her mother laughed, then said, 'I'll tell your father that he can get out his guns.'

Andrea laughed. 'Mom, I know this virus. Don't get exposed.'

'We'll be safe, dear. I know you'll find a cure.'

'I'll do my best.'

On Friday the thirteenth, the university announced that they were closing. The director pleaded with the administration to allow the lab to remain open. The administration agreed to allow volunteers to continue the research on SARS CoV-2, but whoever stayed was on their own. The only hourly staff to remain would be Roy, the security guard.

The researchers who wanted to stay were Andrea, Director Williams, and two graduate researchers, Christy and Dave. Together, the four went to the store to get the things they would need to shelter in the lab.

On Friday evening, Kyle sent her a message, 'My company laid off all non-essential personnel today. I'm out of a job.'

Andrea took a deep breath and messaged back, 'Then stay home. And tell your friends to stay at home.'

‘Sean cut all ties. He believes that it’s unprofessional to remain friends with people who have been laid off,’ Kyle texted back.

‘Good, you have no reason to go out. Everything you’ll need for the next two months is in the closet.’

‘TWO MONTHS?’ Kyle sent back.

‘That’s the minimum I think it will take for the virus to cycle through. Please, for us, stay home.’

‘You’re the expert,’ Kyle texted.

Andrea fed and took care of the human tissue cultures. Growing these cultures was critical for the experiments. Separating them and exposing the new cells to SARS CoV-2 in a consistent manner provided a dependable test medium.

Dave and Christy worked with the mice through all phases of their life: mating, birth, raising, infecting, treating, dissecting, and then disposal. Henry took over the imaging systems. All four of them reviewed the images, as they had time during the day. The results were written up and posted online.

Every substance they tested in the hope it would kill the virus was important. The many that didn't help, or even increased the infections, were ones that other labs did not have to test.

On Easter Sunday, Andrea decided to chance going to the apartment to get more clothes and other supplies she needed to stay at the lab. When she arrived Kyle wasn't there, and the apartment was a mess. She knew Kyle didn't like to clean or cook. It was apparent he went out to eat and avoided doing laundry. She sent a text to Kyle: 'I came home to pick up some things. Where are you?' Then she gathered her things.

She noticed that some of her stuff was out of place. In her gut, she had this creepy feeling that she was in someone else's apartment. Her senses switched to investigation mode. There was a mug half-filled with black coffee on the counter.

Kyle always added milk or creamer. She checked the fridge: one carton of fresh milk, and one expired. Then the evidence came alive: dirty plates sat on both end tables, and the remote was on the right table. Kyle always sat on the left side of the loveseat. Then she noticed that the bed was made. Kyle never made the bed.

Andrea immediately felt like anything she touched would infect her and make her sick. She grabbed her bags and ran out of the apartment. She started to walk up the street when the text from Kyle came: 'I'll be there in less than a minute.'

She looked up and down the street: no Kyle in either direction. Then she turned to the apartment building and caught the eye of Rachael in the window of the apartment across the hall before she slipped out of sight.

Kyle came running out of the apartment building. 'Andrea!'

She took a step back. 'Social distance, Kyle.'

'Hey, can't we still hug?' Kyle said,

holding out his arms and stepping forward.

'I've been working with the virus, and you haven't kept your distance from others,' she said with a fierce glare.

'Just watching some movies and sharing meals with others in the building,' he said.

'You have been sharing more than that. When did you start making the bed?' she asked in an irate tone.

'It's not what you think,' Kyle pleaded.

'Go isolate,' Andrea commanded. 'Box up the rest of my things and put them by the door. I'll pick them up later.'

'Let's talk this over.'

'You don't get it. The last four weeks is nothing. This is just starting. Social distancing needs to last for months,' Andrea said in a louder voice than she ever used with Kyle. She started to drag her suitcases towards the university. 'Rachael needs someone right now. I don't.'

'Andrea, stay. I love you.'

'I know,' Andrea said over her shoulder without looking back, more to hide her tears than to show rejection of Kyle. The mile-long walk to the university was the loneliest walk she had ever taken.

Roy let her into the building. He was a typical security guard who played video games, watched Netflix, or read books most of the time. Andrea knew Roy went home to an empty apartment every night, but worried that he didn't keep his distance from others. She never went close to him, and made sure that the food and groceries he brought in were sanitized thoroughly.

The rest of April became a blur of days. She made and infected tissue samples, then monitored the growth of the virus and added drugs to test their ability to slow the infection without affecting the tissues. Then the team repeated anything that showed a better than an average reduction in viral growth. If the results were encouraging, they would repeat the experiment while varying the doses. Everything was documented so they could share the results with other universities around the world.

She kept in touch with her parents. They were responding to emergency maintenance requests of their renters. Her father felt like it was his duty to help anyone who called during the lockdown.

By the second week of May, the team focused on two promising substances.

Andrea was sure of the effectiveness of one potential drug. She wanted to accompany the drug to whatever laboratory picked it up for additional research, but the isolation regulations made it impossible. She had to let the potential cure go.

As had become her norm, Andrea remained in the containment area until after eight in the evening. As she showered Christy shouted, 'Andrea, your phone has been ringing all afternoon.'

Her mother had left many messages.

'Mom, is everything all right?'

'No. Your father is ill. He's resting

now. I know he has the virus.'

'Have you called the doctor?' Andrea asked.

'Yes, we're following the instructions. I hoped you might have something to give him.'

Andrea thought about the potential cure. She had no idea of the dose or how she would give it to her father. 'Mom, there are possibilities, but a hope here in the lab to a drug that can be given to anyone is a long process.'

'You have to do something!' her mother pleaded over the phone.

'I've done all I can. The recovery rate is going up. If Dad has trouble breathing, call 911. Doctors know how to treat this,' Andrea said, trying to be encouraging while her concern for her father sent her gut into a spiral.

'I prayed you would have a cure before we got sick,' said her mother.

'Researchers around the world are working on a cure. We needed more time,' Andrea said as she slumped to the floor next to the lockers. 'I needed more time.' Tears flowed down her cheeks.

The next morning Andrea's father was taken to the hospital. Her mother was distraught. She wanted to be with her mother, but that would mean stopping the experiments and a ten-mile walk through town. Her longing to be with her parents clashed with her fear of exposure and her drive to find a cure. She went to her cot, curled up, and tried to sleep.

Every call Andrea made to the hospital gave the same report, 'Your father is in ICU, and we are doing all we can.' She would then call her mother and give her hope. Two days later, the hospital forwarded her call to a grief counselor.

She called her mother. When her mother answered, Andrea heard only coughing. 'Mom, can you talk?' There was more deep coughing. Andrea called 911 for her mother.

She called her mother back. 'Mom, help is on the way.'

Between coughs, Andrea heard, 'Cure

me, Andrea. Come cure me.'

Andrea knew she was like so many others who prayed, hoped, and fretted over loved ones fighting for their lives against a lifeless foe. Andrea called every morning for five agonizing days before her call was forwarded to a counselor.

SARS CoV-2 had won the battle with her. The five-story science building containing the bio-lab become her jail. The cold walls of the empty building offered only echoes of her footsteps as she paced the halls. She shunned the condolences of those around her. They were failures, like herself.

What am I working for now? Andrea asked. Her motivation died with her parents' deaths. To keep the research going, she couldn't take a day off. If their schedule got disrupted, it would be difficult to get the workflow back.

Andrea had no idea of the date or what day of the week it was when the announcement came: a company had developed a working therapeutic. Andrea searched for the details online. It was an inhaled drug that could be administered every four hours for three days. The active ingredient was not the one she'd found, but similar. She had been close. Her parents had needed to avoid contact for a few more weeks.

The next day Director Williams terminated all the experiments and left the building. Andrea watched Dave and Christy joyfully dance down the street, hand in hand.

Roy gave Andrea a ride to her parents' house.

'Call me if you need anything,' Roy said as she got out of his car.

'I don't know what I need.' Andrea sighed. She stepped to the front door and went into the house where she had grown up. The silence brought her to tears. Memories of her happy childhood flooded her mind. She stepped outside to the back patio and envisioned her mother and father in the chairs where they would come to relax. She pulled up a chair, watched the sunset, and contemplated about how a bat in China had taught the world about the butterfly effect.

WORLD WAR C

Nick Carlson

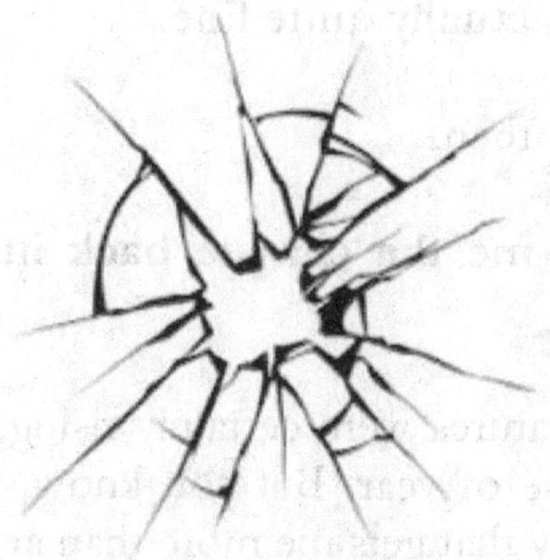

[Nov. 7, 2020. TALLAHASSEE, FL. With the oncoming winter, cases are expected to flare up again, confirming all experts' early speculations that we'd see seasonal fluctuations, much like an influenza strain. How many years this will continue, is anyone's guess. Jimmy Henshall certainly seems to have low expectations, and I don't blame him, considering all he had been through, both the incident and the resulting media drama. If he's feeling cynical, however, he hides it underneath a relentlessly loquacious demeanor.]

Sorry if I talk a lot, by the way, I talk when I'm nervous.

That's actually quite fine.

Alrighty then.

Regale me the climate back in those days.

Temperatures were certainly rising, it was that time of year. But you know, it's the humidity that gets me more than anything. Feels like you're swimming through a brick wall.

I meant the *social* climate.

Oh. Well…you remember, right? It was an election year – one halfwit bozo against the other halfwit bozo, smacking each other with their walkers. Just like all other cycles, am I right? They've been like that as far back as I care to recollect. Constant, vicious cycles. Never-ending. I've been through my fair share, enough to rattle any man.

…You're eighteen years old.

Right, that's practically my whole life! But anyway, how could you worry about the coronavirus when the real disease was misinformation? Top scientists contradicting each other, elected officials mouthing off trying to preserve their electability, celebrities just absolutely – remember that one bitch? [NAME WITHHELD FOR LEGAL REASONS], blew her head off? On a livestream? I think that was when people started taking things seriously. Self-isolation, quarantine, social distancing, the works. So many memes, so much drama. Jesus.

Was it difficult for you?

Not really. First time I heard "No groups of more than ten, stay six feet apart, only leave for essential purposes," I was like "Oh, so, I don't have to change my lifestyle at all? This is fine, this'll be fine." So when the mayor ordered the countywide lockdown thing, I didn't think much of it. I'd just hide in my room and come down to raid the fridge or whatever.

What about online schooling?

Oh, it was hilarious. Half the time the instructor couldn't figure out how to work his webcam so we'd just be staring at him from the nose-up for like thirty minutes. We all made a private chat and just started shitting on him in there. A good two thirds of the "class" always disconnected early – which sucks now that they won't graduate, I mean, the material was easy enough, you'd rather sink your participation grade than just sit there and get through it? I get it, but, I mean, come *on*, are you really going to do that? Probably why that one guy, Brandon something-or-other, pulled his dick out on camera that one day. Probably went a bit stir-crazy and thought it'd be funny. I think that's when the instructor decided to switch to individual assignments.

How about the rest of your family?

[He looks away]

...One thing at a time? Your mother?

My mother treated the whole thing like it was an...extension of her job, if you know what I mean. She was a stay-at-home mom, that was her job. If keeping clean and using common sense and all that stuff were her normal routine, it was upped to eleven during this whole scare. Always cleaning, always making sure we washed our hands, calling up relatives, slapping us if we touched our faces. **[He shows me a scar on his cheek]** That was her ring finger. She also made the grocery store trips. I went with her once, and it was terrifying. She was like the Terminator. Objective: Toilet Paper. Target: Sighted. Target: Acquisitioned by third party. Response: Fuck you, asshole.

And your father?

He drank the Kool-Aid, and dashed it down with Jack Daniel's. Started parroting every byte of conspiracy theories radio and television put out there. Only the old people would die and that would save the economy. Everyone in the White House had it and was passing it along to the rest of Congress. Started calling it the Wuhan virus, the Chinese virus, then when he was informed that was "racist," he settled with the "totalitarian-authoritarian-communist-shitbag virus." **[He rolls his eyes]** It was insufferable. Having to work from home wasn't doing him any favors, so that's how he vented, by ingesting and vomiting back up all the information he could, no matter how errant. So it was a no-brainer to stick to my room.

How did you all hold up?

Just kept to ourselves. Took each other's crap on the chin and then forgot about it later. Sure there were fights, some of which involved me, but again, nothing dire. I think we all knew in the back of our minds that there were bigger things out there and our petty squabbles didn't matter. It just wasn't worth the energy. And did I tell you how bad the humidity was?

So…what happened then?

…

Can you start from the beginning? When you first started realizing things were about to…head south?

…

What was he like before?

Like any other kid, I guess. Hyperactive, annoying, mouth going a million miles an hour. And this is important, I realized – DJ had no frame of reference to compare this whole debacle to. Too young to read much or watch scary movies, so this whole thing was like…a novelty, I guess. I thought it would just be another wrench in his day, yet another thing to go off about, asking questions and talking.

But it didn't stay that way.

I should have seen it coming months ago, when then-candidate [NAME WITHHELD FOR LEGAL REASONS] came by his school and lectured the whole class about climate change, telling them they only had twelve years before it was too late, telling them something had to change, that they were the only ones who could do it… Imagine one of the most powerful people in the country gracing your first grade class with a visit and then basically telling them they're fucked unless they did something about it. I see stuff like that at my age and I just roll my eyes and pass it off as another political stunt. But when you're six? I can very well see how a kid might misconstrue something like a pandemic after all that.

He started out just as I thought he would…asking questions and talking. God, I can still hear his high-pitched interrogative tone in my head. Mom tried her best to answer him but she never really read or watched the news either so it was just more common sense stuff. And of course Dad wasn't much of a help either. So after about a week of lockdown he took to his room, with his tablet, just…laying there, silently, doing the reading himself. No context. No filter.

[He's silent for a long time]

He comes down from his room during dinner one night, and he stands on his chair and makes an announcement. Says he's going to take discipline into "his own washed hands," and christens himself the "Toilet Paper Poobah." Says he's going to help Mom with enforcing safe practices. "Every time I see someone doing things not allowed, I'm gettin' rid of one toilet paper." Mom of course says that won't be necessary, but DJ ignores her and rants about how "there are others less fortunate" and "we have too much toilet paper for our own good." I laughed because, you know, I thought it was funny. The whole thing was stupid little kid antics. And he gives me, I swear to God, the most convincing evil eye I've ever seen, and he says, "Dead men don't do much laughin'." Mom grounded him of course, but obviously such inconveniences as "groundings" wouldn't phase the Toilet Paper Poobah.

How did he start out?

Little things…by comparison, anyway. Every time one of us went to wash our hands he'd hover behind you like a gremlin and just stare. He was mouthing to himself. Timing you. Probably singing "Happy Birthday" to himself, like everyone was suggesting you to do. Later though, you started forgetting that he was there. His voice became a whisper in the background, like a ghost… Then, it became a part of your mind. Indelible in your subconscious… In those moments, the only thing you'd know is the running faucet, the sound of wet flesh sliding against itself, and his voice…in your head. **[His eyes widen; his tone takes on a high whisper]** "Happy birthday to you, happy birthday to you…"

You weren't worried at first?

It was so stupid, man, c'mon. I had my brains in order, I had two other adults in the room – a six-year-old kid couldn't just twist you like that because he had a crazy idea and we were all stuck in the same house. …But then again, that was all only the first few weeks.

Did he deliver on his promises?

Oh Hell yeah. Mom forgot to wipe down the fridge after opening it one afternoon and he just takes a perfectly good roll of toilet paper and drowns it in the sink. He got grounded again, of course, but by then it was too late, and we were down a roll. And really think about it: what the Hell was a grounding going to do? We were all pretty much grounded already. Everyone had their own shit to worry about, and that slippery little bugger took advantage of that. He snuck out and watched from the sidelines, hiding in plain sight. He got caught obviously, but every time he got dragged up to his room he would scream about "repression" and his "first amendment rights" and "justice for all" and how "no one soul could crush the

Poobah." And all this coming from a kid who got a C+ in Reading.

And then?

…

Take your time, it's okay.

Mom got sick. Don't know if it was COVID or not. Just…developed a cough. No tightness of the chest, no fevers or chills, none of that, just a standard garden-variety cough. But of course DJ took notice. Took a roll of toilet paper and wrapped it around his nose and mouth like some tactical ninja, and spied on her. Making sure she always coughed into the crook of her arm and then wiped it down. Whenever she'd leave the room he'd rush in and spray and scrub the area she was sitting in, to the point where the walls would bleach and the colors on the upholstery would fade.

You saw all this happening?

Second-hand mostly. From both Mom and Dad. Saw it once, watching TV. But I'd gotten to the point in my life where I could tell what was going on just by reading their faces. And of course I could hear everything going on and deduce things. DJ's room was blocked off by his bookshelf. He was hoarding cleaning supplies. Every time I walked past his door I caught a whiff of chemical agents. You'd swear he was brewing depressants in there, but he was just scared. Scared and determined.

Weeks passed like this. We'd already lost three rolls of toilet paper because of him, we were down to the last one. We deliberately cut back on food so we wouldn't, you know, have to go as much. Tensions rose, we were all weak and irritable and hungry. So hungry. But not him. Pure mania was keeping him up and running. All those necessities like food and water and sleep became afterthoughts. It was at that point when he wasn't DJ anymore. He had crossed the line, overstepped into some dark alternate plane of being. [Long pause, then a laugh] Listen to me, I sound like goddamn Lovecraft. But there's literally no other way to describe it.

And then that day.

That day. Yes. Certainly, "that day."

Do you not want to talk about it?

…

I understand. The journalists said enough already.

I'll tell you. I will.

Take your time.

[Another long time passes]

Dad coughed. And I don't know if it was just a cough, or whatever Mom had, or even COVID itself. I guess I'll never know now. But he's just sitting in his home office, typing away, he coughs…and DJ rushes past me toting Clorox spray like a freaking handgun. The kid is *trailing* toilet paper. It's wrapped around his limbs, his head, it's tapering behind him like some deep-sea creature. Runs into Dad's workroom and just starts engulfing him in the stuff. Dad of course sputters and coughs some more and starts cursing at DJ, calling him a damn idiot, telling him to get out of there, but DJ was…relentless.

Probably would have kept spraying until the can ran out or Dad disintegrated, whichever came first. This whole thing I did witness, by the way. I was there. Dad swipes blindly at the air and strikes DJ, and the kid comes crashing to the floor. Crying at the top of his lungs, the toilet paper shredded from his face, I could see his cheek reddening from where I was standing.

Mom comes barreling in, hysterical, yelling at Dad, coughing, trying to pick up DJ…but he squirms out of her grasp and sprays her in the face too.

"Germ-spreaders! You all are sick! Sick, sick, sick!" Both distracted, that's when he makes his final escape to his room. I remember his eyes, bloodshot and shiny with tears. Wet toilet paper clinging to his skin like dandruff. He looks at me and screeches, "A pox on us all!" Then slams his door shut

.

He was *gone.* Just absolutely *gone.* Mom and Dad fought again over him. Dad had to bust his door down but all DJ did was curl up in the corner and giggle. Dad howling,

Mom praying, DJ gone berserk, and what do I do? Lock myself in my room, like I've always been doing.

Fuck, man, I mean, what could I have done? Some kind of sappy bro-to-bro talk like in the movies? Nope. That doesn't work in real life. Once someone is gone, they're *gone.* Not like I would have had the time to try and pull something like that off anyway. Maybe if three days had passed and it happened, then you could've blamed me for not trying. But no. Quarantine had made us all on the edge of our ropes. I literally didn't have the time to try. It was evening, I was hungry, I was delirious, I thought the best thing to do was sleep, and start anew in the morning.

[Long silence]

I later read that the reason why most people die in...scenarios, like that, is because the smoke dulls their senses, and they just suffocate in their sleep, not knowing what's happening. Our smoke alarm was functional, but the bastard must have taken out the batteries during the night. The only thing that woke me up in time was the sound of…her…she was screaming. Pleading. Desperate and vain. I jolted to my feet and immediately breathed in smoke. I ducked my head by instinct, I only coughed a few times. The door handle was hot, so I kicked it open with my foot. DJ's bedroom was directly across the hall from mine, that's clearly where the fire had started. It was just a…a portal in there, like staring at the surface of Venus or something. Smog and flame and black crumbling ash, vague shapeless forms that used to be his bed and his toys and everything…I could feel the heat dig into my skin. But I heard another cry, and I staggered down the hall to my parents' room. There were embers in the carpet, burning my feet…fire danced up the walls, encompassing me. Hazy and noxious and scorching. Crackling noises like splitting wood. Their door was already open. I…

[He chokes up. Puts a hand to his temple]

It's almost comical, telling it to someone else. He was using the…the damn cleaning spray, as a flamethrower. Just laying it…laying it thick on their bed…blue flames caking the mattress...Dad, he must have...must have already, been...Mom was, writhing, this Mom-shaped silhouette...crusty and ashen and...she...gurgled...

[He sobs, head dipping while his composure slackens. After a moment he pulls himself together]

And he was just standing there. So deliberate. Ensuring that every square inch of their room was...cleansed. That must have been why he did it. Got that sick idea that fire was the ultimate cleanser. Probably thought the whole house was riddled with coronavirus, and it was up to him to "purify" it. Because only he could do it. Because it was all up to him. Because the world would have been fucked otherwise. Sound familiar?

The kid was burning up too, the toilet paper had already incinerated, his clothes were glowing orange, his hair was...devilish. Hades from that Disney movie, but horrifying in real life. When Mom stops moving he turns and looks at me. He has to shout over the roar of the flames. "You have it too!" I bolt. The stairs are right there. It's unbelievable, the instinctive speed you can move with, when you realize your life is in danger. I don't remember flying downstairs, or crashing through the window, tumbling over the holly bushes…what put me back in reality was the glass in my skin. I crawled through the lawn, the glowing orange windows in my peripheral vision, the smell of smoke…the blood seeping down my body and aggravating my burns.

He followed me. Came through the window, completely ignoring the broken glass, holding a chunk of flaming wood. His hair was gone. His skin was alternating raw and cooked. Smoking and flaming like a goddamn comet from outer space. He was taking his time. Like one of those Komodo dragons, you ever seen that video, them stalking that buffalo? Just very slow, like he knew there was no hope. And he was right. I couldn't move. There *was* no hope. I started crying, sobbing like a baby. It was all just too much over the last several weeks. So much confinement, then the sudden explosion of activity, and then to end it like this? Random and graceless and… He sees me, and he raises the wood over my back, fixing to drive it into my spine, and he says, real low, "Dead men don't do much cryin'."

Something in the house gave, I don't know what, the gas main or something. But it exploded, and the shockwave knocked him back, incapacitated. Just this bright little body flying over me, that's the last I saw DJ. But, again, I doubt that was really him. The last time I saw…DJ, no, not DJ…my little brother…the last time I saw my little brother, was…weeks prior. Before…everything.

[Longest silence yet.]

My God…awful. And the aftermath?

Came to in a hospital bed. The burns, the malnutrition, were top priority, obviously. They tested me for COVID anyway. Guess what? Came back negative. Didn't have it. Wasn't even asymptomatic. Just didn't have it. They broke the results and I just shrugged, like, "whatever." Insurance wouldn't cover the damage to the house, so I moved in with a friend. He's been great.

Didn't have it either, in case you were curious.

Went back to school. I'm doing fine. Thanksgiving's coming up, gotta be ready and be thankful and whatnot. Thankful that my friends all made it through. That the country managed to limp on from all that legislative stimulus package crap. For life, and sanity, and sanitation.

Other than that…not much else I can raise up with my prayers. All do now is just…speculate. I'm not sure I believe in God, but I wonder what He'd make of little DJ. The Toilet Paper Poobah. The COVID Crusader. Having done what he did for health and safety's sake. Because he thought it was noble. Because he thought it was *right*. I don't know, man. What do *you* think?

Honestly, I'm not sure I'm qualified enough to give an answer.

[At this, he gives a grim smile]

Hm. Another one.

THE SPECIAL PLACE

by Ian Neligh

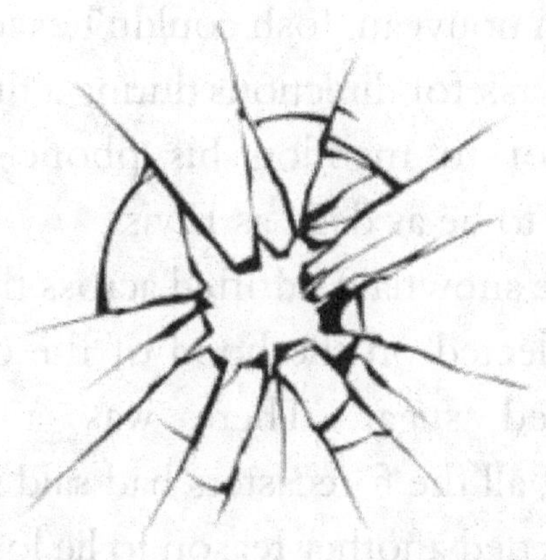

Navigating the empty streets in a borrowed Chrysler, Josh hunted for an address he couldn't find. It was like the property was hiding from him. In the foothills west of Denver the houses were large, the properties giant and spread apart. There seemed no real rhyme or reason to the location of the homes or their addresses.

Through the dense evergreens were houses just short of mansion-sized. Most showed the unfortunate architectural influences of the 1950s. He suspected many were second homes. During the mud season, or in the unlikely event of a pandemic, most were also empty. They were like gaudy mausoleums decorated in

Western nouveau. Josh couldn't exactly get out and ask for directions during a time like this. Not to mention his phone's GPS seemed to be as dead as Elvis.

Fine snowflakes drifted across the road and collected on the hood of the car like powdered sugar. There was a storm coming, all the forecasters had said so—as if he needed another reason to lie low for a while. Jamie had talked him into crashing at a house. She was one of the good ones, one of those that had almost slipped away but stayed in contact. She was selling real estate now and had suggested the plan over the phone. He was stuck on the Front Range with no business, regardless.

He could do well with a little time to recover from the road. He refused at first, out of principle. It was a show, and she remembered it well and insisted, and he agreed. The virus destroyed his business opportunities. He was stuck and needed to stay somewhere. Jamie didn't want him within throwing distance of her apartment. It had something to do with a couple of roommates who were hypochondriacs, afraid he would get them all sick. Whatever, Jamie always had a better idea. Like Josh, she didn't mind bending the rules on occasion.

She told him there was a rich widow's home she was trying to sell. The widow lived somewhere in Florida now. She needed the dough to pay for an expensive retirement community. Josh couldn't imagine what it was like to retire; he felt like he would hustle for the rest of his life.

Jamie said the real estate market tanked when COVID-19 reared its ugly head. There was no reason he couldn't stay in the widow's house.

'At least until this all blows over,' she said.

The proposition didn't sound half bad, and he agreed. Jamie said she would come over and quarantine herself with him once she got away from the office. That turned a mediocre idea into a great one. If he could find the house. She gave him directions, but Jamie had to repeat herself twice. Josh got easily distracted while driving with the music on.

She also gave him a shopping list and sent him some money through his phone for groceries. She knew him, knew it was feast or famine when it came to his bank account. These were lean times, and money-making opportunities were rare.

After mulling over Jamie's suggestion, he agreed. He liked to think of himself as an opportunist. He then took her financial offering and spent it in a grocery store almost as empty as its shelves. His last job was to sell a couple pallets of surgical masks that had 'fallen off' a truck. He always believed you had to look out for yourself when you could, no matter the state of things—and money was money.

A driver he worked with before alerted him to a deal where he would work as the middle man. All he had to do was arrange a quick turnout in a parking lot west of Council Bluffs, Iowa. The pay wasn't great, but he grabbed a mask and slipped it into his pocket. Josh later wore it while shopping. He felt self-conscious with it on as he strolled down the aisles, looking for Jamie's various odds and ends. He walked past the other late-afternoon shoppers with rags tied to their faces. Josh felt conspicuous. He knew he'd soon get over it, as he did most things. He paid the exhausted checkout lady and practically skipped his way out to the parking lot.

In a car that wasn't his, filled with groceries bought with money he didn't earn, Josh was looking for a house he didn't own. That was fine by him. If he could find it. When it seemed he might not, he felt his good cheer drain. He looked again at the address on his phone's map. It was working again. Driving at a crawl, he went down the forested road. He tried to remember if odd- numbered houses were on the left side or right side. Josh swore at the bags of groceries in the back seat as more snow collected on the hood. Only one in three houses seemed to even have an address visible from the road.

He idled past a house with yellow trim

at the far end of a long driveway. He went on past a few acres of forest and a house made to look like a ski lodge. Rolling his eyes he drove on, glancing at his GPS, then stomped on his brakes, his seatbelt growing taut. The phone's map had come to life and told him he was right in front of the property. Peering out the passenger window, he spotted a narrow dirt driveway leading off of the street.

'Well, howdy fucking-do,' he said, then turned the steering wheel all the way to the right. He accelerated off the road and up the long driveway.

Pine needles scraped along the sides of the Chrysler as he made his way along. After about twenty feet he came across a large two-story house made of river rock. Like everything else in this neighborhood, it was outdated. But not without its certain charm. The kind of place Willie Nelson and Kris Kristofferson might have hung out at when they were living in Colorado during the '70s.

There was no car out front and Josh

parked, then texted Jamie he had arrived. He'd have the afternoon to himself—Jamie said she wouldn't arrive until after dark. He got out and gathered up the groceries, trying to remember if she'd said it was the front or back door she'd left unlocked. He tried the front door and found that it opened, and pushed his way inside. It was decorated just as he thought it might be. Lots of dark wood paneling, thick coffee-colored carpet, and partial walls filled with etched yellow glass bricks. He got the chance to eye some of the house as he hurried his way past the decorated living room. There were some photos, an ancient television, and other dated bric-à-brac. On the wall near the kitchen was a rustic piece of wood. It had too much varnish and the words 'A Special Place' charred into it. The house hadn't been updated since Jimmy Carter was in office.

He shouldered open the old Sears refrigerator and stuffed everything inside. There were some expired condiments on the shelves, which he shoved to one end.

That done, he dug a beer out of a plastic bag and took a look around. A couch with faded floral arrangements sat in front of a television with enough wood on it to build a damn barn. He walked across the carpet to the TV and clicked it on, surprised by how long it took to come into focus. But it eventually did, and the picture was in black and white. It was a rerun of an old show. It took a moment for him to recognize it as *The Dick Van Dyke Show*. Josh laughed out loud and walked back to collapse on the couch. He made some phone calls and did his best to try and plan for a time when the virus didn't have everyone homebound. After getting a second beer, making another call and watching part of an episode of *Gilligan's Island*, he got up to look for the bathroom. While in the hallway, he turned up the massive gold thermostat. The house was chilly and the temperature outside plummeting.

He trekked down the carpeted hallway, past a small stairway to the second floor. A parade of bad art in giant wooden frames greeted him before he found a door leading to the small bathroom. Flushing the toilet, he made his way back to the television and watched an episode of *Bewitched.* Jamie texted him she was on her way. Good, it felt a little weird to be in someone else's house. Having company would be a great remedy. He watched another episode.

Watching the ancient TV shows of a time when America was doing fine made him feel uncomfortable. He turned it off and dug through a box of vinyl records under an old turntable. Music was just what he needed. His fingers flipped through the covers: The Carpenters, Fairport Convention, Linda Ronstadt, and Joni Mitchell. Groaning, he put on The Carpenters. He then went to the kitchen to make a sandwich from groceries he'd purchased. The snow was really falling now. He could see it collecting in the pines outside the window.

Josh hoped Jamie could get out of Denver before it piled up too much. Karen Carpenter's voice in the other room creeped him out for some reason. Hadn't she died in the early '80s of something like heart failure? Chewing, he went over to the record player, changing the record out for Joni Mitchell. As the needle dropped, he noticed a small bookshelf with several photo albums. Putting his plate on the carpet, he sat down and pulled one out. It was faux leather, and the plastic laminate holding the photos in was brittle and cracking. Most of the pictures, as he suspected, seemed to be from the '60s and '70s.

The photos showed men and women with long hair, bell-bottom jeans, and headbands. Many scenes captured partying around Colorado at different locations. In some yellowing shots they were skiing or in a large meadow or dancing in someone's living room. Josh looked around—this living room. He kept flipping and found one thing consistent in all the photos. There was always a dark-haired young woman. She wore thick eyeliner, had long bangs and ramrod straight hair going down her shoulders. There was something about her he found unsettling. Josh wondered if she was the widow who was selling the house.

As he continued to turn the pages he realized that there was something off about the people in the faded color photographs. They were doing something in the pictures, not just partying, dancing, and smiling for the camera like in the decade before. There were candles and what looked like some type of ceremony in some. In one blurry photo he saw a naked woman and something that might have been a knife. It was hard to make out. Squinting, he saw it was the brunette. There was what looked like a bloody handprint on her arm. The loud buzzing of his phone on the coffee table caused him to jerk away from the photograph.

'Jesus,' he swore, crawling over to it on his hands and knees. It was Jamie.

'Hello?' he said.

'It's me. I'm making my way out of Denver, but the roads are bad,' she said. 'I should be there in a few minutes, I think.'

'Okay,' he said. 'I'm already settled, got the food and everything.'

'Sounds good—see you soon.'

'See you then,' he said, hanging up.

Jamie sounded distracted. The roads must really be in bad shape. He slid across the floor back over to the photo album and turned the page. There were no more photographs. He was contemplating pulling another photo album off the shelf when he heard it. His heart jumped in his chest and seemed to hold still, knocking the air out of his lungs. Someone had just walked across the floor above him. Forcing himself to breathe he strained to listen, but only heard Joni Mitchell's eerie guitar-strumming ballad 'Help Me'.

Josh stood, looking at the ceiling, waiting for any further noise. He realized it was likely his imagination, or even more probably the old house settling. No one had been inside for some time, and houses were known to do that. Plus, he had turned up the heat. The house had been cold for months. There was no one there. Jamie had been inside last evening. Even still, he found himself walking down the carpeted hallway to the stairs leading up to the second floor. It was stupid he hadn't at least given the second floor a look when he got there, and he might as well do it now. Joni Mitchell's high, wavering vocals played behind him as he walked up to the landing. He turned, looking up at the second floor. It was already getting dark and he was thankful to find a light switch near the top, which he flicked on. A dim yellow light lit up the hallway and the doorway to four rooms beyond.

'Hello?' he said, feeling like an idiot, walking to the first room.

'Is anyone home?' he asked in his best Boris Karloff voice. No one responded, not that he expected anyone to. He glanced in the first room and found it was trashed. Garbage and art supplies lay all over the floor. Frowning, he moved to the second room. Peering inside he saw it was possibly a small library, but all the books were in great dusty piles. He shook his head. He didn't mean to tell Jamie her job, but at the very least she should see this place cleaned. The third room had a single stained mattress on the floor and about a dozen melted candles lying around it. As his mind worked to process this last thing, his phone buzzed in his pocket. He was getting texts from Jamie.

Where are you?

He scrolled to the next message.

I'm here, where are you?

He texted back: I'm at the house.

There was a long moment before she responded.

The house with the yellow trim?

Josh was still moving to the last room and reading this message when he stopped. The house with the *yellow trim*? Was that what she had told him when he was on the phone getting directions earlier?

He took a step back, away from the last room. This was a bad idea. He no longer wanted to take a look. Before he could do anything more, someone's fingers reached out from inside the room. Slender and white, they held on to the doorframe. Then he saw black hair and a young woman's grinning face creep ever so slowly around to peek out at him in the hallway. It was the same girl from the photographs. He opened his mouth to say something when his voice caught. Like a spider, she came for him down the hallway. Through the acres of trees and snow separating the houses, no one heard him scream. But even if they could, no one was home.

out from inside the room. Slender and white, the [illegible] door frame. Then he saw black hair and a young woman's [illegible] slowly around to peek [illegible] hallway. It was the same girl from the photographs. He opened his mouth to say something when [illegible] [illegible] [illegible] [illegible] [illegible]

THE CLIMB

Juan Ozuna

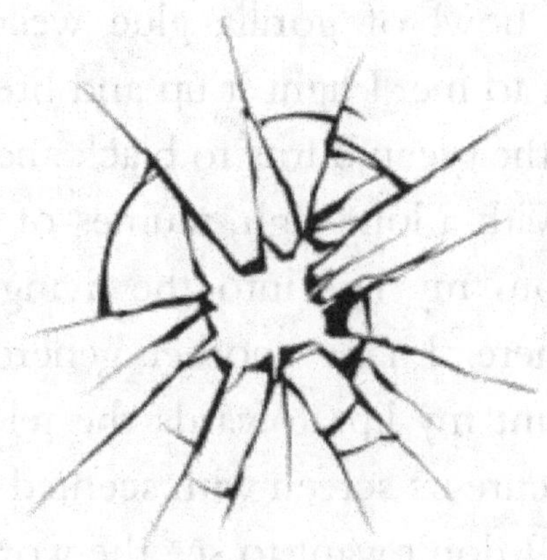

1,705 people died yesterday, and that's just in the United States. The daily death counts are ticking upwards again, more people becoming gasping lumps on white hospital sheets struggling to catch their breath every agonizing second until their last.

I worry that soon I too will be a death statistic.

'Bro, you'll be O.K. Just relax,' David, my roommate, reassures after I voice my growing belief.

'It's not fine. The world is ending, and this is just one of the many ways in which Mother Earth intends to rid herself of *us*,' I say.

David just shakes his head and loads

another bowl of gorilla glue weed then passes it to me. I light it up and breathe it in until the green burns to black and white ashes. With a long sigh, plumes of smoke float from my lips into the living room atmosphere. I take another generous hit then point my lips towards the television and obscure its screen with scented clouds because I don't want to see the world, not like how it really is.

When the marijuana clouds disperse the news is again in view.

On it is our president saying how successful he's been in leading the war against the 'China virus', as most states plan to let their stay-at-home orders expire within a week.

'That dude's a snake,' David says. I turn to David and see the sun-burnt skin of his arms and jaw flexing. I know he has family some in this country, including our leader, would label as 'illegals' and I feel the hate emanating from him towards this man on the screen, towards this liar.

And right now he's lying, I think,

that the country will get better.

I turn back to the screen, to the president, and imagine a slim tongue slithering between his thin, pursed lips and beady reptilian eyes sunken in his puffy, orange face.

'Yes, he is indeed a snake.'

Because of the high, I stare at the orange serpent for an indeterminable amount of time until I hear David at my side breathing deeply. I turn and am surprised to not see him taking a hit from the pipe, but instead, just breathing intently and holding his chest.

'You good?' I say.

'Yeah, I'm cool, just need some fresh air.' He doesn't look at me as he says this. He instead hugs himself and shuts his eyes as if he's trying to quell a panic attack.

'Let's go for a hike! Plenty of fresh air up in the mountains,' I say, trying to distract him but also excited at the idea of leaving the apartment. During weeks of quarantine, it's felt like the place has been shrinking around me. The mountains, I hope, will also alleviate my fear after weeks of being fixated on daily death counts.

'Sounds good,' David agrees.

***

A few trails have opened again to the public, although they do limit the number of people allowed at a time. We park off the side of the road and walk towards our trail's beginning when David and I hear the familiar yells of a friend.

'Y'all ready to hike this mountain or what? Damn, you guys smell like weed! Y'all get any on you?' says Isais, one of our more obnoxious friends. Not my favorite person, but he was David's friend before me, and David had insisted that we call him up to meet us at this mountain.

We begin the hike at a steady walk, but stubborn pride makes us increase our speed; if one of us got ahead, the others would want to get ahead of that person, and so it continued, this race to be first until we all three were sprinting up the mountain's imperfect steps.

'Last person to reach the top is a pussy!' Isais says.

We all then scramble quicker up the steep incline. We shove each other aside and out of the narrow path so that we must hurdle bushes and avoid cacti. We bound up steps and sidestep other hikers abruptly. Isais almost knocks over a lady hiker and lady hiker yells obscenities at him for it. He just laughs but David and I kick at his shins to shut him up and we continue, lifting leg after leg up that mountain. A couple times I slide on loose rocks and leave a piece of my shins on jutting boulders that stick up from the dirt like misshapen teeth, but the pain only incites me to climb more viciously, my breath a growl.

'Last one up has to take a cactus up the ass!' David says.

This threat is not taken lightly. David used to lie down beside sleeping homeless men and whisper lullabies while caressing them. To catch a ride, he'd jump on the hood of a car and hold on tight, and even when the car would speed and swerve,

David would grin and press a middle finger to the windshield. So, it wasn't far-fetched that he might snap an arm off a cactus and try jamming us in the ass.

I determined not to be last. And I could tell the other two did as well. Our group speed somehow increased despite trembling thighs and stressed knees.

Neck to neck I don't know if I can outrun them, so I divert upwards from the meandering man-made path, cutting through prickly vegetation that slices into me. I can hear Isais hollering 'Cheaters!' behind me but I ignore. I just run upwards until a point where the climb steepened so much that I had to crawl like a coyote on all fours, rocks stabbing into the soft tissue of my hands. The earth crumbles behind me, tiny avalanches of stone.

I notice my heart is thumping harder, my whole body is tremoring. I look to my hands as they grip the red dirt – they are purple and tremble. Panic shoots through my veins.

Am I having a heart attack? The thought panics me even more. No, it's just the weed that's making me paranoid. It must be?

I try to compose my breathing into a steady, easy rhythm, until I notice holes in the mountainside wide enough to fit my arm through.

As I pass over these countless holes in the Earth the wind picks up, blows more fiercely, puffing up rust-colored dirt clouds. I picture people buried within the mountain and the holes I am climbing over lead to their gasping mouths so they could breathe and continue in their torment. Their collective souls inhale and huff as I rush up the mountain. The wind blows against me as I struggle to get away from those opening, stretching hand and foot forward until the ground levels enough to where I can stand. I run, until my nose and chest burn as I devour the mountain air. It smells dry and bloody.

A hissing. I hear a long gesticulating tongue, but from where I cannot discern.

Is the snake warning me or taunting me? I turn every which way but am unable to spot the damn beast. Blood drips from the crease of my lips. I realize I'm clenching my jaw, so I relax and open and still more crimson gushes from my mouth. Some meat lolls loosely between my teeth. *My tongue! I've bit into and separated part of it.* At this point, I wish I'd brought some water as I choke on the congealing spit and blood in my mouth.

In these moments of blood-letting and hallucinatory stimuli, brought on either by drugs or the engulfing anxiety of these past weeks, or both, David has put distance between me and him, and I still cannot catch my breathe.

Isais, I need not worry, for he trudges still on the mountain trail behind me. I can only see the top of his black-haired head moving slowly. Perhaps he's given up?

'Come on. Don't be a bitch,' David yells from his advanced position.

I decide to ignore my quivering hands and labored breathing. The bones of my sternum drum, hit by a mad heart, but still

I climb. I am no bitch.

While sprinting upwards my vision blurs and sweat stings my eyes. My body is part stumbling, part-running now. Tree branches grab at my arms insistent that I stay. Some animal takes a bite out of the side of my right foot, but when I look down to inspect, all I see are the needles of some small cactus I stepped on protruding from my shoes. I pull these out then run.

And am soon caught up to David much to his dismay. He punches me and I punch back. We grab each other by the shirt collars and pull each other towards the ground but our strengths are nearly equal, so we remain afoot and continue kicking and pushing dangerously close to the edge.

We approach a part of the mountain that looks to require strenuous effort to pull oneself over. To the left of us, the mountain does not slope, but rather drops off swiftly more than a few hundred feet. As I stare out over this perilous ledge while running, David sticks out his foot and causes me to tumble.

I fall to me knees. And David, he keeps on going, tossing himself up and over the ledge until he is standing triumphantly above. He smiles. But his face distorts, the smile turns into confusion. He's gripping his chest, and leaning over, now tripping off the mountain's edge and down out of sight.

I peer quickly over the edge from my vantage point, and watch David being torn apart by the mountain. He flops helplessly like a bag of garbage whose contents spill out and litter the mountain's facade.

He can still be fixed, even though his arms are falling off and his legs twist unnaturally, even though his head lolls loosely from his neck, striking rocks and leaving splatters of blood. Despite it all, he can still be fixed. I believed this, foolishly, until David hit the flat earth and sank into himself.

Blackness enveloped me as my consciousness receded into itself. Minutes later I awoke to hellish scream and scorching brightness. *Am I in Hell?* My vision slowly cleared, revealing the mountain and with it my memory of David's fall returned.

Isais then arrives. He yells although I do not understand his words. I am just staring down at the smeared remains of David.

Isais may have called for a rescue team because I can hear chopper blades now. But there's no one left to rescue. Just many bits of someone to scoop up. I've been staring at the remnants of David, waiting for him to get back up and walk around, hell, I'll even take flopping around, since his body is now a flattened mess. I'll carry him if I have too.

'I'll carry him,' I tell Isais and the rescue team before I black out once again.

***

After the biopsy we learned David died due to the coronavirus. The doctors say he must have had it for a couple weeks. I try to remember if he ever complained of fevers or shortness of breath or any other symptoms, but David was a stubborn person. If he felt the symptoms, he kept it well hidden.

Isais and I were warned to isolate at home until tests became available for us.

Home is where I've been this past week. It's much more spacious without David's presence. More room for gloom.

I haven't slept much since the hike. My blood pressure is too high, the blood pumping too furiously to allow any kind of relaxation. Anxiety has been my only feeling, that and grief. When I lay down despair blankets and smothers me. The skin of my face sizzles like a frying pan is underneath it. I gasp and choke. *Is this the end? Shall I shut my lips and pinch my nose to expedite the inevitable? The torture is nerve-wracking, this out of air feeling.*

And then there are the few times when my shaking body can no longer withstand its sleep-deprived state, and it is then when I slumber...and when I do finally rest is when I have the most vivid dream. A recurring one. In it, I am falling, indefinitely, flailing from the mountain bluff and David is falling next to me even though he is already a dead, flattened mess. We both descend towards the mountain floor, but it cracks and rough, crumbling lips part. The floor inhales us and we're then falling through a vast tunnel through damp earth lit by the faint glow from the sunlight above us. The tunnel is slick with blood and a maroon mist drenches us as we tumble down past walls branched with limbs that reach out and scratch us. There are holes in the walls and when I peer into them I discover they lead to open, spasmodic mouths, opening and closing, sucking desperately. They seem to notice me and shout. The cries of those trapped souls ring through my ears like a choir of misery. David is beside me, unspooling through it all, entrails flailing behind him like crimson streamers. His face is a pale grimace, and when he turns, I see the back of his head is missing, those pieces of him grazed off and left behind. We fall further until the sunlight dissipates and we're then falling through darkness, with only the rough aspirations of the people in the walls to overwhelm my senses. David and I continue falling until the fall grows mundane, and I allow the rushing air to whip and bend me like my friend's broken cadaver. We fall through heavy darkness that whispers sinister things. It says, 'Death is near.'

Then I wake. Breathless and sweating.

***

David is cremated, and since his family still refuses to accept their son's untimely demise – ululating loudly and refusing to touch the black vase that is a skin for his ashes – I steal David from his family's living room after they invited me over for dinner. I don't want his family to suffer, I stole David because I knew he just wanted to breathe in some fresh air.

I take him and bring him up the mountain, back to the spot where he last stood. A black vase serves as a skin for his ashes.

I overturn the vase and a breeze scatters David's ashes, picks them up and tosses them with the air currents. The gray and black specks spray my face and layer my skin, seeping into my pores, into my mouth. He tastes like sand.

Looking out over this edge, I think I might know what David was feeling in his last moments, because I can feel it now too: Perhaps his vision blurred, obscured by lengthening lights, his pulse beat irregular, chilled limbs trembled at his sides, going numb. Then David's oxygen-starved mind lost grip of consciousness, and he fainted, fell over the cliff's edge and plunged down below.

But *I* don't black out. Maybe I will soon though. I haven't taken the test for Covid-19 yet, but the fear is always there. The fear itself might be what breaks me. I feel like I'm already falling, becoming disfigured along a mountain's face as the floor rushes up to end me.

I think this disease destroys the mind

first before anything else. The seams of me seem to be tearing, my sanity is splitting. My chest feels heavy.

Even though I'm in the open, mountain air, I lean over and try to catch my breath but it is fleeting, and the sky is spinning. David's ashes drift all around...I don't know if it's my imagination, but I think I hear David calling me. No. Screaming. His soul is being tossed violently in the air and he is screaming.

I shiver and listen.

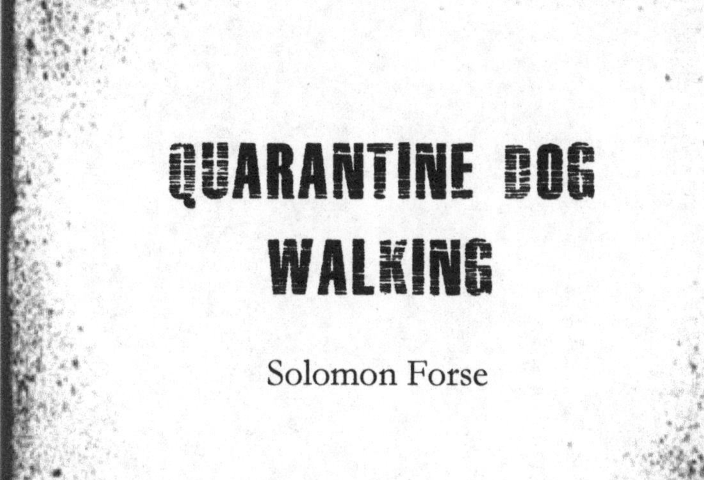

QUARANTINE DOG WALKING

Solomon Forse

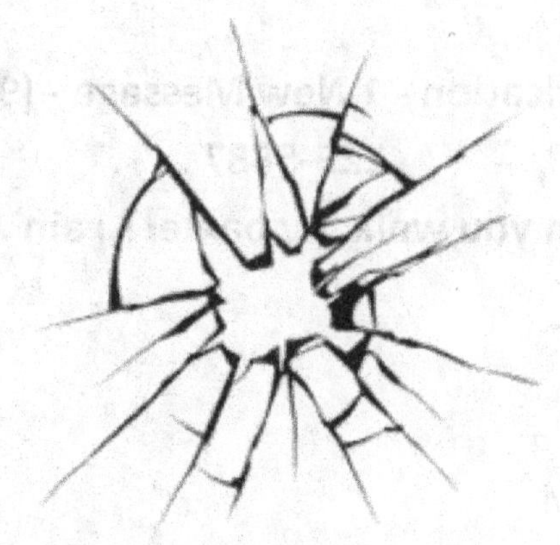

CL > community > pets

Quarantine dog walking

Posted 1 day ago

Hello, anyone in downtown I would be happy to exercise your pups! I charge just $20 for an hour walk, and for hikes on location it is $40, lasting 1-2 hours. I have great references, and will pick up from you. Picture attached.

-Leila

- do NOT contact me with unsolicited services or offers

post id: 6995401498

#

Notification - 1 New Message - (916) 225-5887

can you walk my baxter? i am ...

#

6:35 AM

can you walk my baxter? i am a senior and too worried to go out.

this is janet

7:47 AM

Good morning, Janet! :) This is Leila. I am pretty booked today with all the quarantine families and helping my sister, but I can give you my last slot at 7:30pm if that is not too late.

8:00 AM

that is fine

sorry i dont want to make contact.

can you come inside to get baxter tonight?

i can leave the leash for you

8:01 AM

Of course, that is no problem given the circumstances, Janet. So one hour for $20?

PayPal or Venmo is preferred, but I can take cash. Tell me more about Baxter.

8:05 AM

ok i will hide a key under mat with some cash

bax is a mix. he's a real love bug

address is 7748 n 4th st.

and i will stay in my room

8:07 AM

Thank you, Janet. Just to be sure, he's not under any breed restrictions and doesn't have any aggression problems?

8:11 AM

no no. he is old and slow like me.

he will love you

can you feed him when you get here too?

8:17 AM

Sure, no problem. He will be nice and happy for his walk then! Just set everything out for me, please.

9:12 AM

how much do you weigh?

9:15 AM

I'm sorry??

9:18 AM

bax is old but sometimes he gets excited

a young thing like you might get pulled along

9:20 AM

Ohhh. Yeah, I'll be fine. Let's just say the panic-buying at the grocery stores isn't stopping me from eating three hearty meals a day! And I do CrossFit. I might be a young thing, but I'm strong ;)

9:21 AM

perfect

and no symptoms leila?

9:26 AM

Of course not! I already work from home with my main business, so I have had little contact with the outside world as it is.

I am looking forward to meeting your little Bax! I will text you this evening when I am on my way!

9:28 AM

Thanks

#

Notification - 1 New Message - Baxter (Janet)

are you still coming? youre late and ...

#

7:31 PM

are you still coming? youre late and bax is hungry

7:33 PM

I am so sorry, Janet. I am on the way! I was walking my sister Ashley's pup and the little guy gave me some trouble. I'll be there any minute.

#

7:38 PM

Omggg Ash you won't believe the house I just pulled up to. It's like Hoarders meets Amityville. And this old lady left me wrinkled bills from the 90s or something. Like what Dad gave us for our allowances when we were little kids. I'm def washing my hands.

7:40 PM

Be nice, Lei-lei!!! She probably has no one else

And honestly if she had the virus she would be dead already

Mom is freaked since all the victims so far are seniors

But yeah TOTALLY wash your hands to be safe lol

7:41 PM

Good point. And we definitely need to watch over Mom.

7:42 PM

Aaaand it gets better. 'Janet' literally forgot to leave the key. I have to call her now. I'll let you know how it goes later tonight. Bye!

7:43 PM
Kk you be nice! :)

#

Baxter (Janet) missed a call from you.

7:44 PM
sorry cant talk i lost my voice
whats the matter

7:45 PM
Hi, Janet. Again, I'm so sorry I'm late. I'm out front. I found the envelope under the mat but there is no key... unless I'm blind :)

7:46 PM
oh sorry. i accidentally left the key here in my room
well i cant get up right now
i can slide the key out my bedroom window. ok?

7:47 PM

No problem, Janet. Do you mean one of these windows out here?

7:47 PM

no can you come around back? im sorry

7:48 PM

Umm okay. No worries.

7:50 PM

Hey Janet, the fence is locked. I can't really see out here.

7:50 PM

if you slide the trash can to the fence you can climb over

7:51 PM

Okay...

Just a minute.

#

7:51 PM

So, Ash. Remember way back when you all made fun of me that summer because I couldn't hop the fence to grab the ball from the neighbor's yard? Well yeah. Here I am again.

7:51 PM

Wtf are you doing Lei-lei??

Are you still at the old lady's house?

7:52 PM

Yeah. I guess she can't move, so I have to go to her bedroom window in the back to get the key. But the fence is locked. She literally just told me to climb on a TRASH CAN and jump over. I feel sort of terrible about abandoning this lady and her dog ... but yeah Ash, this is straight sketchy.

7:53 PM
Okay facts
But just imagine if it was you and you were 80
And you needed someone to feed and walk your lil Benny boy

7:54 PM
True.

7:55 PM
Okay, I just peeked over the fence with my phone light, and it looks like freaking Jurassic Park back there.
It smells like the zoo, too.
And no, it's definitely not the trash can.

7:56 PM
You don't think there would be any snakes or anything? I really want to get back in my car...

7:56 PM

Don't you leave that poor little old lady!! Of course it smells, she can barely take care of herself

And it's still technically winter, so no snakes I think. Just watch your step and breathe through your mouth

Send me pics of her pup when you're all done!!!

7:56 PM

Ugh. Fine. I guess you're right.

I will send you some well-deserved pics of Mister Baxter in one hour!

7:56 PM

Baxter? He sounds cute already!

I might have to wait until tomorrow to see them tho

Ryan is coming over ;)

7:57 PM

Be careful... the store might be out of N95 masks but they sure as hell have condoms in stock ;)

7:57

Okay Aunt Lei-lei

7:58 PM

Don't even joke about that...

I have to go, though. Janet probably thinks I'm dead by now.

7:58 PM

Don't forget. DOG PICS!!!

#

7:57 PM

leila are you in the backyard?

7:57 PM

No, not yet! I had to move the trash can. It was really heavy.

Oh, and Baxter is inside, right? He won't come out a doggy door and think I'm an intruder or something?

7:58 PM

no there is no doggy door

7:58 PM

Okay.

8:01 PM

I made it over.

8:01 PM

Janet, where is your window? I'm using my phone light but I can't see through all the bushes.

8:02 PM

Are you sure Baxter isn't out here? I can hear something.

Janet?

8:03 PM

Sorry. I'm going home. I'll put the money back under the mat. I hope you understand, Janet.

8:03 PM

wait wait

dont go. i really need you to help him

please im desperate. no one else will help my little bax. hes so hungry

just stay along the wall you will find the window

8:04 PM

Okay, okay. I’m looking.

8:04 PM

Where is your window?? I can’t go any farther along the wall.

8:05 PM

Umm there’s a HUGE hole in the ground and it’s in the way. Did I miss the window somehow? I’m confused.

Baxter (Janet) missed a call from you.

Baxter (Janet) missed a call from you.

8:12 PM

Janet. Hey, this is embarrassing, but I think I fell down that hole. Please come outside. I can't get out.

8:13 PM

Can you hear me?? I'm yelling

Baxter (Janet) missed a call from you.

8:14 PM

Janet, please come out!

Ashley missed a call from you.
Ashley missed a call from you.

8:16 PM

Ash pick up the fucking phone!!! I need you to come get me like right now

Ashley missed a call from you.
Ashley missed a call from you.
Ashley missed a call from you.

8:18 PM
Janet please I'm trying to climb out
I'm stuck down here

Baxter (Janet) missed a call from you.
Baxter (Janet) missed a call from you.

8:19 PM
I seriously can't get out
I keep sliding down
It smells so bad I can't breathe please

Baxter (Janet) missed a call from you.

8:20 PM
If you don't come in one minute I'm seriously calling the cops

8:20 PM
im sorry leila
there was nothing else i could do
the stores have been out of meat for weeks

8:21 PM

??? Please please I am so scared there is something down here like snorting or something

8:33 PM

im sorry leila

god forgive me

#

Notification - Phone - Ashley

6 Missed Calls

Notification - 1 New Message - Ashley

Lei-lei pick up the fucking phone I'm ...

#

Notification - 1 New Message - (916) 555-0163

Hey there, do you have any openings for tomorrow at ...

IS IT TUESDAY AGAIN?

Sabrina RG Raven

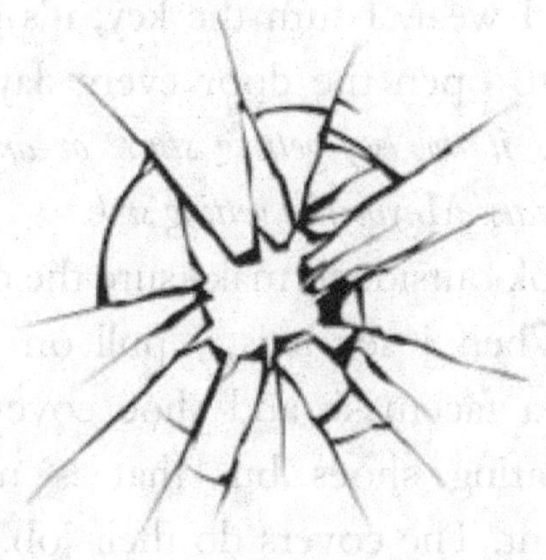

I sit in the dark looking at my phone. It's my only contact with the outside world, but it's gone quiet. I've messaged friends, tried to call but no one has replied in days. I couldn't tell you how many days mind you. It's been a blur. *When was the last time I'd eaten anything? When did I shower last?* I sniff at myself. *Not that it mattered.* Can't go outside. We have to self-isolate. There is a virus.

I hear footsteps on the stairs. I pull my blanket tighter around me and cover my head. There's a knock on the door, then a thud. Then the footsteps retreat again. *It must be a Tuesday. Food delivery is on Tuesdays.*

I go to the door, still cocooned in the

blanket I wear. I turn the key; it's getting harder to open the door every day but *I wonder is it the key getting stuck or am I just getting weak. Maybe I'm getting sick.*

I look outside to make sure the coast is clear. When I see it is, I pull on rubber gloves, a facemask and shoe covers. I'm not wearing shoes but that is nothing important. The covers do their job. I pick up the crate from the stoop and rush it to my kitchen. I only order things in packets now. You can sanitise packets much easier. I tip all the packets into the sink and return the crate to my front step.

After all the groceries are sanitised, I dispose of my safety gear and wash the bench and floor – anything I've touched. I need to shower.

***

No one is replying to me still. I've called my mother a hundred times this week but she never answers. I mash buttons on the television remote but my tv isn't working anymore. I check my social media but it shows nothing new. It's just the same information on food rationing, deliveries and how long they think we're going to be locked in.

How many days has it been?

***

I hear footsteps and a knock on the door.

Is it Tuesday again?

'Hello?' I hear a voice call. 'Can you hear me?'

I ignore the voice. *It might be a trap.* Maybe someone is getting desperate. The food rations aren't the biggest. Maybe someone wants mine too. Food delivery people never talk. They knock and drop. That's protocol. Protocol is to keep us safe.

'I know you're in there. We need to talk. We can talk through the door.'

I turn around and go to my room. It is small, but it is mine, nonetheless. I wrap my blanket around me tighter and cover my head. The voice is muffled now. I can pretend it is just the couple next door. I can just hear them talking through the wall, that's all.

The knocking is all in my head. I am safe here. Finally it falls quiet.

***

I don't know where my phone is. My one lifeline. Not that anyone was replying. What if they're all dead. What if they all got the virus and died. I haven't heard my neighbours for a while. I'm not sure how long it's been.

I hear footsteps and a knock on the door. *Is it Tuesday again?*

'Hello? Can you please just come to the door?' the voice calls. 'It's okay. You don't have to do this.'

It is a trap. I knew it.

'Come on! I know you're alive. I saw you bring in your groceries.'

He'd been watching me.

'Daisy, open the goddamned door!'

How does he know my name?

'Daisy, I know I don't have a key, but I will call the police if I don't get an answer from you. You need to talk to me.'

I hadn't heard my name in such a long time. Daisy. I am Daisy. How does this man know that?

He knocks on the door again, hard enough to make it rattle on its hinges.

'Daisy!' he screams.

'Go away!' I bellow. My voice cracks a little. I've done very little talking apart from to myself in a hushed voice. I cough to clear the roughness in my throat.

'Just come to the door.'

I shuffle a little further down the hall towards the door.

'It's me, Daisy.'

My name again. It stops me in my

tracks. I drop my blanket and reached for the side table up from the door. I used to drop my keys here when I got home from work, before the virus. The wooden bowl of fruit is caked in a layer of dust. I stare at it. *How long has it been?* I grab the edge of the table and begin to push it towards the door.

'Daisy, please open up. It's been two fucking years. Where did you think the groceries were coming from? Who's paying your bills?' the voice cries over the squeaking of the table legs on the floor.

I paused. *Two years? Had it been that long?* I shake the thought from my head and give a final shove at the table until it thuds into the door. The metal dish next to the fruit bowl crashes to the floor, spilling my keys and a handful of loose change around my feet. The wooden bowl of fruit wobbles, sending a dust coated plastic apple to the floor to roll its way down the hallway.

'Go away,' I mumble at the voice before picking up my blanket and retreating into my room.

***

Where is my phone? I need my phone.

What day is it?

How long has it been?

***

The knocking wakes me from my sleep. *It must be Tuesday.*

'Daisy, I have the police here with me. You need to open the door. Please.'

It's him again. Is he going to take me? Have people descended to kidnapping and looting? I don't want to get sick.

'What do you want?' I call. It barely sounds like my voice anymore.

'Ma'am, you need to open the door, or we will open it ourselves, with force if necessary,' comes a second voice.

There's a gang of them. I run to the kitchen and grab a knife. I doubt I could do much damage but I go back into the hallway, holding the blade out in front of me.

'I've got a knife!' I call.

'Put the knife down, ma'am! We are coming in.'

'Don't hurt her,' I hear the man say. 'Please, she doesn't understand what's happening.'

Then the thuds begin. The door rattles: the table upending to send dusty, plastic fruit flying down the hallway around my feet. The wood begins to splinter, then the door crashes open, sending the table skidding down the hall towards me. I drop to the floor and cover my head, the knife clattering to the floor, as two men with guns run at me. I start to cry. Then I feel arms wrap around me.

'Daisy,' the man says, 'Daisy, it's me. It's Joey. Your little brother. It's okay. The quarantine ended over 2 years ago. It's safe. You're safe. It's over.'

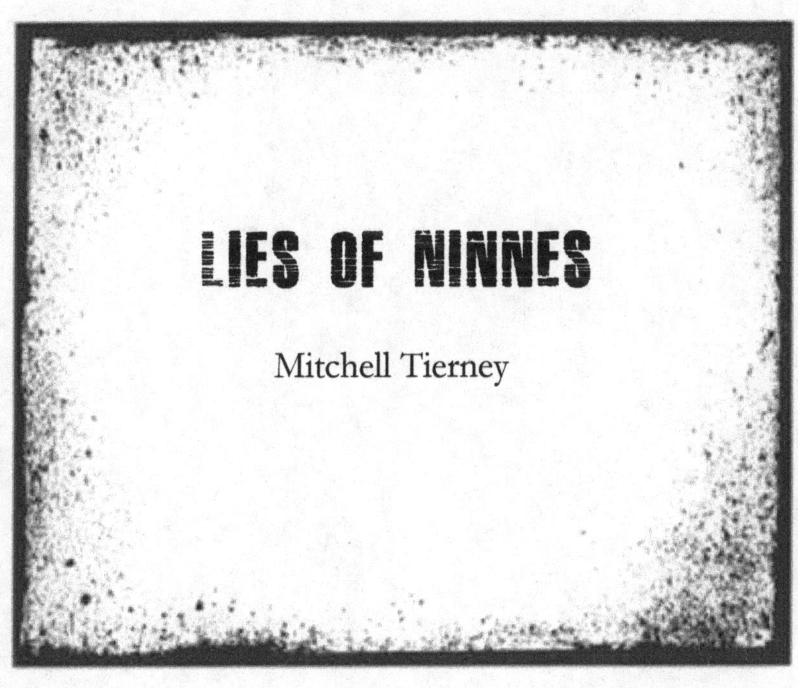
LIES OF NINNES
Mitchell Tierney

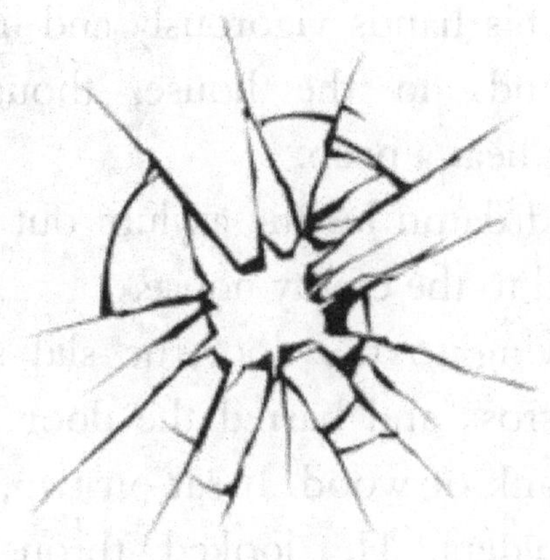

The sound of staggered thumping and a boot hitting the door echoed through the hallway. There was motion from upstairs, but they stayed perfectly still. As instructed. Keys jangled and finally the door was open. It was kicked again by a large boot and swung against the rear wall. A man appeared. He wore scuffed jeans, a long sleeved shirt and his hair was matted, long and disheveled. The one they called 'Eddie.' He shuffled in quickly, arms full of bags and a mask covering his lower face. He kicked the door shut and dropped the bags on the ground, swearing and tearing his way through the house to a large bottle of sanitizer on the kitchen bench. He washed his hands vigorously and listened for sounds in the house, though he couldn't hear a peep.

'God damn lunatic asylum out there!' he yelled to the empty house.

Moving to the door, he slid several locks across and barred the door with a large plank of wood. It sat on two, heavy iron holders. He looked through the peephole. Not one car on the street. He picked up his bags and took them to the kitchen. Tins of peaches, beans, a bag of rice he had found under the stand, several light bulbs, a length of rope someone sold him in the car park and marker pen. No vegetables, no fruit and especially no meat.

'It's all but bare out there. No one and nothing. Shelves are empty, people have either gone into hiding or moved on,' he told the kitchen as he started to unpack.

His pantry was stocked with tinned baked beans, brown rice and cans upon cans of soup. He added to his collection and recounted it. On the pantry door was a piece of paper. He crossed out the old count and added the new one in. There was a thump from upstairs and his eyes rolled up his sockets, staring at the ceiling.

'Son of a bitch,' he grumbled.

He ran to the foot of the stairs and snatched a baseball bat leaning against the wall, dried blood already on it. The handle was wrapped up with black tape, and the end was dented. He took to the stairs, two at a time till he reached the second-floor landing. Three doors, all still and quiet. Large chains and bolts holding their contents safe from the outside world. He stood and listened, one ear to the left door. There came the sound of garbled muttering and then someone being hushed.

'Make her quiet,' Eddie said, tapping the baseball bat on the door. 'Make her quiet… or I will.'

It stopped. He turned left, then suddenly let out a heavy cough. Buckling forward, he dropped the bat and fell to his knees, gripping his chest. The cough was harsh and tore at his throat. Spots of blood splattered the ground. He looked at them, and darkness reigned down around him. His head spun and everything he had feared, everything he avoided was suddenly here.

There was a knock at the door. Eddie snapped his head around, wiping remnants of blood off his bottom lip. He ran downstairs, leaving the bat by the right-hand door. Looking through the peephole, he could see two people in full hazmat suits standing on his welcome mat.

'What do you want?' he yelled. One of them held up an ID tag.

'We are from the department of Disease Control, are you Mr. Ninnes?'

'What do you want?' he repeated, yelling through the door, his eyes pressed against the glass.

'We've had record cases of the virus in this area and we've been sent to ask each house if they had been to any supermarkets, or convenience stores in the last 24 hours?'

'Who asked you?'

'Sir?' one of the control agents looked

at the other. In her hand she held a small testing kit, and in the other a fresh swab.

'Who asked you to check each house?'

'The Department.'

'No, it's just me here… and I haven't been outside in days.'

'Sir, if you experience any difficulty breathing, coughing and fever, please call the helpline. I'll place the information pack in your letterbox.'

'Okay, okay,' Eddie said, banging on the door with an open palm. 'Do that and leave.'

He felt the itch climb his throat. A spittle of blood burst over his lips and sprayed the back of the door, and over the glass. Now the agents were seen through a filter of red. Eddie stepped back, gripping his chest.

'Sir? Are you okay?'

Eddie coughed uncontrollably. His throat felt like an apple covered in razorblades was trying to make its way out of his mouth. He choked and fell backwards.

'Sir! Mr Ninnes?'

***

When Eddie woke, he was on the floor, staring up at the ceiling. He could see the bolts he put in all those years ago. He sat up and felt dizzy. His hands felt swollen and he had to suck in air in order to fill his lungs. Gripping the couch arm, he stood on shaky legs and felt his brow. It was hot and beaded with sweat. He went to his icebox and fetched a jug of water, emptying it in several long gulps. Something heavy dropped upstairs, thudding and rolling across the floor. Without waiting to listen further he took to the stairs like a possessed animal, digging into his pants pocket and retrieving a ring of keys. His head was still dim and fuzzy as he approached the doors.

Several chains were thrown to the floor, followed by the slide and click of deadbolts. Lastly, a large iron bar was yanked off its hooks and tossed aside.

He kicked the door in and stormed into the room that smelt of urine and faeces.

Body odour and sweat filled his nostrils as he marched into the rancid room, where a girl was chained up in the corner. She had a sheet draped across her body, with holes bitten into it then torn to create slots for her arms. Her leg was chained to the ground. He stomped over to her and grabbed her by the hair. His neck pulsated with veins and the skin on his cheeks turned beet-red. His left hand clenched into a fist. His teeth gnashed together as he pushed his face into hers.

'What the fuck was that noise? What have I told you?' he screamed, spittle flying between his teeth and splattering over her face.

'It wasn't me,' the girl whimpered, flinching away from him. She pulled her chain close to her chest. A metallic umbilical cord bolted to an iron clasp on the ground.

Eddie snapped his head to the side. In the opposite corner was another girl. She was cradling a baby. It was gently suckling at her bosom.

'Don't come near us, Eddie!' she shouted. The floor was scattered in old food scraps, plastic bags full of waste, maggots and hundreds of flies. They buzzed with vibrating abandon.

'Give her to me,' Eddie said, stifling another cough as he stepped menacingly towards them.

'Get back, or I'll stab you,' she said, pulling out a sharpened plastic knife.

Eddie stood up, coughing into the crux of his elbow ditch. 'Where did you get that from, Kelly?'

'I made it, now back off,' she said, her voice commanding and abrasive.

'What's going on out there?' the other girl said. Eddie glanced over his shoulder.

She was hoping to draw his attention back to her. He looked at her and smiled, blood on his teeth.

'It's a virus,' he said matter-of-factly, his lips pursing together.

'You're lying,' she said. Her voice never waivered.

'I wish I were, Kate,' he spoke softly,

as if some switch had just been flicked to 'off'. He walked to the boarded-up window and stood in front of it, as if he could see through it. 'If I took you outside, you would die in a matter of hours.'

'Stop lying to us!' the young mother cried out. Her child screamed from the abrupt disruption. 'You've told us this for years… it's not true, now let us go!'

Eddie didn't bother turning to her. He simply smiled, staring at the boards.

'It started years ago and grew and grew,' he stated, matter-of-factly. He seemed to derive pleasure from talking about it. 'It travelled from continent to continent, infecting more and more. Hundreds of thousands of people have died. Maybe millions. They've stopped reporting it.'

Kate looked at the other girl, then to the open door.. She mouthed the words 'no.' Kate nodded. 'Look,' she said. The girl looked out the door and could see something on the ground. It was the baseball bat. She mouthed the word 'baseball bat' back to Kate, who looked up at Eddie.

'Eddie,' she said, standing up. She was naked except for the sheet. The brace around her foot was far too tight and she lifted it off the ground to alleviate some of the pain. Large, red welts circled her ankle. She snuck a glance back at the other girl and nodded to the door. 'Tell me about it. The virus… tell us more.'

Eddie smiled. His fleshy fists started to relax.

'It came so quickly. Isolation didn't work. They stopped all the planes, trains and buses… but it was no good. People were being people. They were still going out when told not to.'

'Not you I bet, Eddie,' Kate smiled at him, then motioned towards the door.

Kelly placed her baby on the ground. Every piece Of her soul told her not to but she repressed it with a force of will. If he took it away, there would be no hope. She wrapped her daughter in the blanket and stood, nearly falling back to the ground but maintaining her balance by placing a hand on the nearby wall. Her child squirmed but didn't make a noise. She turned her head to the doorway. It was the first time she had seen outside the room in eight years. She took a step , picking up her chain; carrying it like she carried her child at night when it wouldn't sleep. Her hands soft and delicate, cradling the cold metal.

'No, not me. I knew this would happen one day. I just knew it. I worked at a factory and they told us to keep working until we were stood down. But I didn't. I went straight to the military surplus store and got supplies.'

'What supplies?' Kate said, watching Kelly move towards the door with fearful trepidation.

'Guns,' he said, turning his head towards her. She saw the coldness in his eyes. The emptiness. The severe lack of human understanding or empathy. 'I stock my food, but it isn't cheap feeding you all.'

Kelly looked towards the landing. The baseball bat handle was a foot from the door. Her chains started to snag on the latch bolted to the ground. She looked at her baby wrapped up in the blanket and tears rolled down her face.

'But we repay… don't we, Eddie?' Kate said, placing her hand on his shoulder and caressing it. His eyes changed. The switch flipped.

'If you were to ever get outside, you would die. Trust me, you are better off here,' he said, spinning around to the corner where Kelly and their child were. Piles of rubbish and diapers were piled against the wall. A makeshift bed made of newspaper and dirty clothes lay on the ground, the indentation of years of sleeping evident. His face turned toward the door where Kelly stood holding the bat.

'Put that down!' he screamed, his voice guttural. He bolted towards her, his strides long and in an instant, he was on her, fists raised.

Kelly gripped the bat, fear making her hands shake. She swung for his head, but the sheer size of the brute made the bat glance off him. He gripped her neck, squeezing with all his might. She choked, eyes bulging from their sockets as the bat fell to the ground with a clatter. She kicked at it as Kate ran towards it. Slowly, the baseball bat rolled along the floorboards, snagging on exposed nails and splintered wood.

'You bitch!' Eddie howled, knocking her backwards against the wall.

Kate reached out for the bat but her leg snapped backwards, yanking on the chain. It was pulled so tight it started to peel skin off her ankle. Her fingertips were a mere inch from the bat.

'Get away from her!' she yelled, watchingKelly being thrown around like a ragdoll. Kate took her sheet off from around her shoulders and tossed it over the bat. She stood naked and shaking with terror.

Eddie stood up, his knuckles bleeding.

'Now for you, you bitch,' he wheeled around, readjusting his fists into a ready stance

The bat flew through the darkened room, looking like an inky blur. It took his jaw to the side, disconnecting and then breaking it. Eddie fell to the ground. Several teeth burst from between his lips. A pool of blood formed around his head. Kate stood in shock for a moment while her ankle bled profusely.

'Kate,' Kelly yelled at her, her hands on the wall to help her get to her feet. 'Kate!'

Kate snapped free from her shock.

'Get the keys! Quickly!'

Kelly went to her child, who had started to cry at the furore. Kate searched his pockets and found the ring of keys. Eddie started to moan and snort as he rocked back and forth. She tried the first two and they didn't fit her lock, on the third try the heavy metal clasp unlatched. Joy and relief washed over her and tears ran freely down her face, devolving into bawling over the next couple of minutes.

For the last eight years she had dreamt of taking it off. She ran to Kelly, trying key after key until they found the right one. She held her child tightly to her chest as they headed towards the door. As they pounded down the stairs, Kate turned and looked back up to the other doors.

'Kate, quickly, he might get up.'

'What about the other girl,' she said.

'We'll get help and come back.'

'I can't leave her behind,' Kate shouted. She bolted up the stairs, trying each key in turn. There was a horrified scream from the room in front of her, where someone else had been kept for years. Years without sunlight, without true human contact had clearly taken their toll. She could hear Eddie trying to move. From behind the door, she heard the meek voice of a girl.

'Who's there?'

'I'm letting you out.'

The key slid into the lock. Heavy thumps came from the open door to her left, followed by a gurgled moan. The lock Kate was holding unlatched in her hand and dropped to the ground. She threw the iron bolt off the hooks where it rattled on the ground by her feet. She pushed the door open to reveal a small room that was roughly half the size of the one she had lived in and was long and rectangular. A small girl sat in the corner wearing a stained and torn dress and clutching her knees drawn up against her chest. The dress once bright with blue Iris flowers, now faded and covered in dirt and dust.

'Who are you?' She asked.

'I'm Kate, we need to get out of here, now!'

The girl tried to stand, but her legs gave way and she fell instead. Kate ran in and wrapped her arms around her. The girl held onto her shoulders. Together they hobbled towards the door, but the girls chain pulled her back. The garbling of blood and spit came from the next room.

'Quickly,' the girl said. 'He'll beat us both!'

Kate fumbled with the keys, trying to find the correct one. Just as the lock slid off her ankle, the silhouette of Eddie crossed the door. His jaw was disfigured. It was hanging from each side of his face, as if it had been cleaved in two. He stumbled, his arms outstretched, reaching for them. His eyes were wide, and blood trickled down his head as he fell forward. Replacing his silhouette was the shape of Kelly, child held against her hip and a heavy cast iron skillet in her other hand.

'Let's get out of here!'

Together the three girls ran to the door, sliding all the deadbolts across and pushing the heavy iron sliding panel to the floor. The door opened and fresh air caressed their faces. It was a welcoming sensation. Kate ran out onto the road, the unfamiliar sun heating her skin. She smiled and cried at the same time. From several houses down, two figures came running towards them. Both were wearing gas masks and covered in protective jumpsuits.

'What are you doing outside!' the voice yelped, muffled through thick filters.

Kate's hands went to her throat, 'we were kidnapped 8 years ago…' her throat started to restrict. She looked at her hands to see that they had turned red with rashes. She turned to Kelly, whose nose was bleeding while she coughed blood into her hand.

'Now we're free.'

The sound of paramedics sirens filled the air as the girls clutched their throats. The people wearing protective suits rushed to them, kneeling down and pulling out several gas masks from their belts.

'Put these on, quickly!' one of them yelled.

Kelly slipped one on her child, then herself and lay back against the hard asphalt. She looked up at the sky and once pictured seeing the vast blue emptiness filled with thick, cotton wool clouds. She stared for a moment in confusion. The grey sky was only filled with smog and dark, ashen clouds.

Kate stared out of her mask. The face panel slowly skewing her vision. Her breath fogging up the panel.

'You need to calm your breathing,' one

of the masked women said. 'My name is Susan. Why were you running into the street with no mask on?'

Kate looked up at her and smiled.

'For 8 years I wanted to be free,' she said, her voice almost giggling. 'I thought we were told lies by Eddie Ninnes. But it's all true, isn't it?'

'Eddie Ninnes? The Department of Disease chief Investigation Officer?'

Kate smiled and slid her mask off, lying back against the cradling arms of Susan.

'He wasn't lying, was he?'

The blue and red lights splashed against the faded houses. People started spilling out from their houses to see what the commotion was. The girls were placed on stretches and put into the ambulance vans. The sirens rang out along the streets heading for the hospital as the people returned to their houses, locking their doors and taking their masks off, hanging them on a hook by the door, for next time.

THE CROWNED KING

G. Emerald

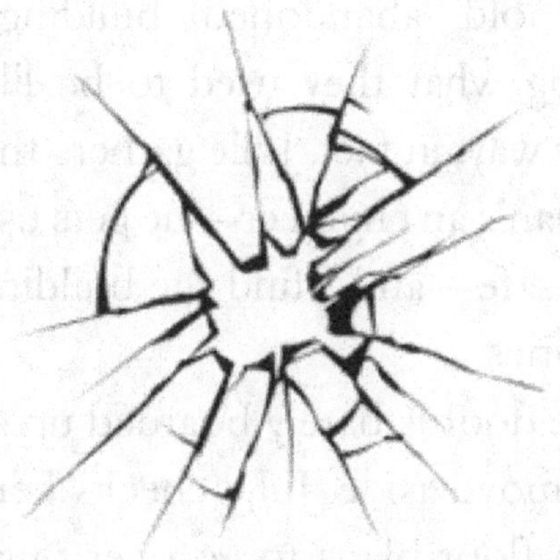

The hospital stands before us, looming though only one story tall. It used to house patients of the pandemic years ago but now only houses debris and out-of-use equipment. Hopefully, it has another occupant—The Crowned King.

History is fickle when researching the pandemic, especially for this place. Not much beyond the Crowned King is found. People report seeing a person's silhouette wearing a crown, hence the name. Most think he's a patient who died here, who proclaimed himself king of the wards and held parades to help cheer up the other patients. He's why we're here.

Urban exploration is our passion.

Finding old abandoned buildings and imagining what they used to be like. We met that way, in fact. Julie gathers the floor plans, Dan's an engineer—he gets us in and keep us safe—and I find the buildings and their stories.

The door is barely boarded up and it's easy to move aside. Julie checks her tablet with the floor plans to go over our route. It's pretty basic: two front rooms then three long wards for the patients, cafeteria, supply rooms, lab, and boiler room. An easy trek, presuming things are fairly clean.

Entering, it's clear that 'clean' is not the case. The antechamber is strewn with debris. Broken chairs with IV poles woven through to hold them together are stacked in front of the doorway, preventing access to the next room.

'Bobby, what happened to this place?' Dan frowns, inspecting the construct.

I shrug. 'Couldn't really find a lot out about this place. I know it was opened in the Spring of 2020 and then closed not long after. I can tell you who supplied the boiler, who built it, but this… nothing about this.'

'Not one mention?' Julie gestures to the barricade, irritated with me for not knowing. She thinks I've fallen down on the job.

Admittedly, I was a bit too focused on the ghost. My cheeks flush and I shake my head. 'Nothing that I read.' It's the truth, though partial at best.

Carefully we make our way over the chairs and poles. Dan looks around the new room appraisingly. 'No sign of internal damage.'

Julie grimaces. 'It's a barricade; they were keeping people in. But why a makeshift one? They have doors and locks.' I can see a shiver run through her, and I have to agree it's an unsettling thought.

Dan strolls by a reception desk, apparently not sharing in the unease. 'Too bad they don't do paper charts anymore, might have provided a clue.' He taps lazily at a long-dead keyboard.

‘Anyone else find it strange that the emergency lighting is on?’ Julie has a point and I kick myself for not noticing. I’d written it off as light from a window but there are no windows, only mild illumination due to emergency lights all around.

‘Eh, probably forgot to take this place off the grid. It’s only using a minute amount so they don’t notice. Weird though, hospitals are usually generator-backed. Maybe they didn’t bother since it was so quickly made.’ Dan has another look around. ‘Still, for something made so fast and for such a singular purpose, they did a good job. Standing well, no cracks.’

‘So glad it won’t be falling down around us.’ Julie pushes forward through to the actual ward. If I didn’t know better I’d say she was trying to get through this place as quickly as possible, which is very unlike her. I share a look with Dan and we follow without comment.

The check-in room was decently-sized but it seems insignificant when we step into the first ward. The room seems to stretch on far longer than the floor plan indicated, beds lined up next to each other against the two long walls with only a curtain to separate them, all pulled back. No sign of any panic here; the room is neat and orderly.

This room demands silence somehow and we quietly drift through the long ward. Dan nudges me and points to a stuffed teddy bear on the floor, rotting with age. It dawns on me that this was the kids' ward.

I lose track of the number of beds we pass, all neatly made up as if the nurses had just been in here. The layer of grime on them says otherwise. The deeper in we go, what little noise we do make echoes back to us. The door to Ward 2 is in sight and it's looking at the door that I spot some drawings. The ward's little art gallery, all crayon drawings of various things hung on the wall. It must have been their only window to the outside world. It seems cruel to keep kids in a windowless room, and I can't help but wonder why they did it.

Dan examines the pictures and I can see the sadness wash over him. He touches one gently. 'I wonder if they made it out.'

Julie looks at him. 'Well some had to or Bobby would have said something; you can't have a hospital with a 100% death rate and not hear about it.' She rolls her eyes. 'What a softie.'

'I hardly think it soft to feel bad for kids cooped up in here with no windows and no outside interaction.'

'What makes you say that?'

He points to a sign next to the door: NO VISITORS FOR ALL WARDS. 'That kinda tipped me off.'

Julie taps a picture. 'Look at this.' We gather in to see. It's a crayon depiction of a man with a crown, the man colored blue and the crown a yellow-orange. 'Here's your Crowned King, Bobby.'

I scan the rest for more. I find two more that look similar—same crown, same man, rendered in roughly the same color scheme. He looks happy with a big smile, but only a smile. No other features. I find another that shows the Crowned King leading a bunch of smaller Crowned Kings in a parade. 'Guess the story of the patient is true,' I murmur to myself. I hope he brought the kids at least some joy while being here.

Julie pushes open the door to the next ward. This one is darker, some of the bulbs broken. We step in and give our eyes a moment to adjust. With a loud gasp Julie shrinks back and we startle at her reaction, looking around wildly. Wordlessly she points and I follow, nervous in both a good and bad way. It's a curtain, and through it I can see the vague outline of a person with horns—or a crown. Unable to stop myself I creep over, ignoring her tug to keep me back. The silhouette remains still. I reach out and grab the curtain, breath held, and whip it back. There sits an IV pole and an old gown hanging on the attached box. My shoulders slump.

Dan comes over and pats me on the back. 'Sorry man.'

I sigh. 'It was too easy anyway.' I turn to Julie, but she doesn't look convinced. I rattle the IV pole a little. 'See—'

I'm cut off by the sound of metal crashing to the floor further down the room. We all jump, panicked. I accidentally knock the IV pole I'm holding as I spin around, adding to the confusion. I don't see anything so I cautiously move toward the sound. The lights seem to dim more and I flick on my flashlight. My beam finally falls on a bedpan lying on the floor. It's metal and spotless.

'It's okay,' I yell back. 'Just a bedpan.'

Julie is shaking her head but follows, holding Dan's hand. 'Bedpans just don't leap to the floor. And bedpans aren't metal anymore, they're plastic.'

She frowns at our questioning look. 'My mom's a nurse, remember? And it doesn't matter; I don't like this.'

I wave it off. 'Like it's the first time we've been scared? Remember the door blowing shut in that school and we ran for five minutes straight?' She nods uneasily.

'Come on, there's still more building left.'

We continue, walking briskly at Julie's insistence. This ward looks roughly the same, just without any stuffed animals or crayon drawings. Still neat and all beds tucked in with hospital corners. What masochist came back here to make the beds?

As if reading my mind, we come upon three beds in a row on the right-hand side that have been disturbed. Bedding wrinkled as if three people had been there, no dust seen. I look to Dan and he shakes his head, getting between Julie's line of vision and the beds. He's right, better to not freak her out further. It's probably just left over from other explorers.

We arrive at the next ward's door, no shadows or jumping bedpans, the unmade beds left far behind. We all sigh in relief as we push through the next door. This ward looks different, the beds spaced further apart with lots of large plastic tubing around.

'This was the vent ward,' Julie says

quietly. 'This is where the worst cases were kept; they needed machines to help them breathe.' We can only nod, and move through even quieter than before. The air here is stale and oppressive, making it hard to get a good breath. The lighting browns out again and is getting dimmer. We are fully in the room now and the door closes behind us with a soft thump. Dan spins around and stares for a moment.

'You okay?' I ask.

He stares for another moment, reaching for the door, but draws back. He nods. 'Yeah, yeah, I'm good.' It feels like he's going to say something more but instead turns and moves on after Julie. I want to ask but know better—it'd just make things worse.

I'm ashamed but there is something I've held back from them, for this exact reason. No one made it all the way through the hospital, claiming something stopped them and scared them away. I can see why but I want to be the first to make it through, a real accomplishment.

Julie is moving through here almost reverently. I've never known her to be religious; I think this is as close as she gets. The emergency lights flicker and we all freeze. 'Think they finally remembered this place is still using power?' Julie asks nervously.

I hear Dan swallow but he speaks calmly. 'Wiring here is probably old and chewed on, no different than that factory we visited. Just turn on your flashlights just in case.' It's good advice, though now we have three moving lights to create shadows where they weren't before. My pulse quickens, trying to keep track of the new shadows, hoping just a smidge that it might be the Crowned King.

We make our way down the ward and it's Dan who spots it first. He freezes and points to the door out of the ward. It's open, waiting for us.

Julie backs away, mumbling 'no' repeatedly under her breath.

I shine my light and find the pneumatic hinge is locked in place, keeping it open. 'Come on,' I say impatiently. 'Probably the last explorers did this. It's nothing.' I press on, ignoring any protests from Julie. Stepping in, I find myself in a sea of tables and chairs. I call back to them, 'Found the cafeteria!'

The kitchen is on the other end, this room fully visible unlike the wards. It's the standard cafeteria set up of so many hospitals. The chairs are a bit strewn about, but nothing out of the ordinary; it's easy enough to navigate around them. I'm almost to the kitchen when a shadow steps into the beam, not dissipated by it, but instead absorbing it! I lift the beam higher and almost drop my flashlight. A head with a crown! It's the Crowned King! And he approached me!

We both look at each other for a moment, unmoving. He waves in greeting for me to follow him. I'm a bit flabbergasted at this. Ghosts aren't friendly, are they? He starts moving towards the kitchen, turns, and gestures again. I speak quietly, words caught in my throat. 'You want me to follow you?'

He nods, my flashlight doing nothing against his darkness. He waves again, this time with some urgency.

'Do you—do you need my help?'

He nods vigorously and claps his hands, excited I understand him. He takes off but I lose him amid the pots and pans. He needs my help! Me!

'Bobby!'

I jolt, brought back to reality.

'I said let's go.' Julie's in the doorway, Dan beside her. 'We need to leave.'

I'm crushed to hear this. The Crowned King contacts me, wants me to follow, and they want to leave? The confusion on my face is plain. 'Why?'

'Something isn't right here. I feel watched and…' She hesitates. 'Something touched me, trying to turn me back. And there are whispers.'

I try to not roll my eyes. 'You're just freaking yourself out. It's a creepy place, everyone agrees on that. It doesn't mean it's dangerous.'

'You're hiding something.' She's looking hard at me, trying to pry the secret out.

I weigh my options. 'No one's made it all the way through because they get creeped out and leave. It's nothing.'

'It's nothing? How could you leave that out?' She opens her mouth but stops as the hanging pots rattle and bang behind me. 'You see?!'

I brush it off. 'It's just the wind.'

'What? We're inside with no windows. Where is the wind coming from, Bobby?' She shakes her head. 'No, I'm outta here. You do what you want.'

'Jules, come back!'

Dan is still looking at me, expression unreadable. 'She has a point, Bobby. There's no way wind could be doing that. And I've been feeling the same. Something is here.'

Before he can say more, a scream pierces the air behind him. We both run, shouting for Julie. Dan reaches her first, the two of them colliding. Julie is panting, eyes wide as he holds her.

'He's there! He won't let me leave!' She points down the ward. 'I saw him! The King wants to keep us here!'

I try to shine my light on it but all I see is impenetrable darkness, absorbing the light. The darkness may very well be him but I don't want to admit that. I don't even have time to think about it though, because wind blasts at our backs and I swear I hear the word 'leave' on it. Julie stands ramrod straight and even Dan is beginning to crack, fear plain on his face.

Julie breaks away from us and shrieks to the room, tears running down her face, 'What do you want from us? Leave? Stay? Which is it?!'

The wind comes harder, pushing us towards the pitch black at the other end of the ward. I realize that the blackness is growing, not shrinking. I'm afraid we'll be absorbed like the light. Something, a cool whisper deep in the back of my brain, tells me the King needs us to move forward, to push back against whatever is fighting him.

'We have to keep going forward, back's not an option.'

Julie's jaw quivers but she wipes her eyes and nods. Dan starts to move as well. The wind is steady and strong but we fight it back into the cafeteria. Once we cross the threshold it stops. Julie sobs once.

I point my beam towards the kitchen. 'There's a door back there, I saw it.' I turn to Julie. 'Pull up your map, there has to be another exit.'

Sniffling a little, she pulls out the tablet. 'There's a door in some room past the boiler room.' A pause and she continues, 'Why don't I remember seeing that?'

We quickly cross the cafeteria and into the kitchen, the door in the corner. Julie still has the tablet in hand. 'This place is a maze. No doors line up the way they should. It was deliberately made to be difficult to leave. Why didn't I see this?'

The question hangs in the air unanswered. There are many things that don't add up. Why build a hospital that's a labyrinth? Why is the Crowned King still here? What was opposing him and why? What about the barricade in the front?

The door leads us to what appears to be a large supply room. It's cluttered with large machines and extra beds. Julie is looking at them cautiously, but with intent. 'These are ventilators. But why would they just leave them here? Wasn't there was a shortage?'

Dan shrugs. 'Maybe they're broken beyond repair? I don't know if they can salvage parts, especially if they harbored a virus.'

She nods. 'Possible.' Eyeing them warily she gives them a wide berth, as if she's afraid the virus will resurrect itself and infect her.

'Hey, look at that—maybe that has some answers!' Dan makes a beeline for a filing cabinet and tries one of the drawers. It opens with a pained squeal and he pulls out some files and starts to leaf through them. Julie and I join. 'You guys finding anything?'

Julie shakes her head. 'Mostly it's

papers from the patients themselves, diaries, drawings, stuff like that. Wonder why they kept it and didn't just shred it.'

We shrug. I feel a small prickle on the back of my neck and try to subtly look over my shoulder. Julie sees it right away. 'What? What did you hear?' She drops the folder she's holding. 'We're getting distracted, we need to leave.' The folder she has spills to the floor and Dan and I bend to pick up the papers.

Dan holds a paper in front of him, squinting to read it in the dim light. 'Huh. 'March 3rd, I see him more every day. He used to be confined to the third ward but I've seen him in the others lately'.' I move over to offer my flashlight so he can see better.

He continues. "March 24th. He is everywhere now, in the cafeteria, the lab, in every ward. We must keep him in. I believe he is the specter of death, not the harmless comfort many pretend him to be'.' A frown and he reads on. "March 30th. I've tried to tell those in charge but they don't listen, they tell me to take my medication. They tell me I am hallucinating but the medication does nothing. I see him now following the doctors and nurses even! He's going to get out!"

"March 31st. I've told the other patients. We must keep him in no matter what. We will barricade him in, even if it means our lives'.' Dan shakes his head. 'It devolves into gibberish after that.' He flips the paper and his brows rise. 'I think he did an artist's rendition of the man he's so scared of.' It's a harsh scratching and scraping of pencil on paper, sharp scribbles that vaguely form the shape of a man, wearing a crown.

Julie's mouth is a tight line. 'We need to get out now.'

'What, some crazy guy mistook the patient in the crown for something bad. He turned the ward against him.' I suddenly feel bad for the King and can see why he might be stuck here.

'The King won't let us leave!'

'Maybe he needs our help.'

Julie gapes at me. 'You've lost your mind.'

When I speak I can't look her in the eyes. 'I saw the Crowned King in the cafeteria before you came in. He stepped right into my flashlight and wanted me to follow him. He needs our help.'

'You saw him and didn't say anything?!' Julie is now beside herself with anger. 'Have you just been lying this whole time? All for some ghost? What is wrong with you?' She spins around and pushes the door, but it won't budge.

'We can't go back, remember?' I say grimly. 'Only forward.'

The wind, that damned wind, picks up again and swirls the loose papers around. This time I can definitely hear the words 'leave now' on it. Papers swirl in a tornado around us. There are more drawings like the one we saw, just as harsh and frightening. Dust flies as well and we cough uncontrollably. The wind then gives a great gust towards the door. It creaks and groans but doesn't budge. The wind stops just as suddenly, ending with almost a sound of disgust.

Julie hits the door once, gritting her teeth. 'Fine, let's go.' She stalks towards the next door. 'But I'm not helping any ghost. I'm leaving, period.'

We follow and the next door opens without issue. This room looks to be a lab and morgue all in one. Biohazard stickers everywhere. Across the room the wall is covered in steel drawers—body storage. The lighting is gone, so we can only depend on our flashlights. I shine mine on where the door might be and I'm correct—on the left wall, as far away as possible from the entrance.

A black shadowed hand thrusts itself into the light and urgently beckons me on. It disappears before I can speak. I must have been the only one to see it.

I turn to find Julie transfixed on the metal drawers. 'Don't think about it Jules; let's just keep going.' She nods stiffly.

Our flashlights go out.

The noise is immediate, not wind this

time but a clattering of metal on metal, drawers opening and shutting, a cacophony that makes me cover my ears just to stand it. Some open quickly but the loudest is slow, with a groan. Someone is getting up. Instinctively I shrink back, neck protected by raised shoulders. The clattering dies down and I can hear something moving, a thump of footsteps in a stiff gait, a soft sigh of a breath leaving a body for the last time. I press myself against a wall. The smell of rotten flesh fills the air. I have no idea where Dan or Julie are, but hope they are safe.

The footsteps stop for a moment. A whimper escapes me and the footsteps turn towards me. I curl into a ball. I feel something in front of me, its stare. The fetid smell is overwhelming and I gag. Something cold brushes against my hand and I cry out.

A blinding flash and all lights are on, fluorescent bulbs included. I'm almost in tears but raise my head. A message is written on the morgue wall in something black and sticky. Handprints surround it in the same substance and I can see footprints also, a set right in front of me. I shudder but heave myself to my feet. LEAVE NOW OR IT IS YOUR FAULT.

Dan is still by the door and pulls at it frantically. The door opens an inch but he is violently pushed backward. Julie runs to help him up. I'm paralyzed. Across the room the door forward slams open, the inky blackness holding it for us. 'See, guys? It's him! He's helping us!' I race for the door and grab it, just brushing against the darkness. It's cool, solid, and takes my breath away. I can feel something on the other side trying to force it closed. The wind has kicked up again much stronger and now I can hear multiple voices, discordant but in unison. 'No! You will not win!'

A hand from the darkness waves hurriedly. Julie stalls where she is, staring at the hand. 'I can't, I can't!'

'Make your choice now, because I can't hold this much longer and I don't think he can either!' I shout harshly over the din. It's no time for second-guessing.

'No, I won't.' Julie slips to the floor, hopeless. Dan looks between the two of us wildly, then runs towards the door. He just makes it past and I shoot in behind him. The door slams hard, shuddering. It's a terrifyingly final sound. Dan throws himself on the door, beating his fists on it. 'Jules? Jules, are you all right? Say something, anything!'

There's nothing. No wind, no voices. Nothing.

The solid darkness has receded and the lights are dim but the room visible. It's the boiler room, except there's an extra machine.

'A furnace,' Dan says. 'Cremated their dead here.' The furnace whirs to life with a great hum. Dan's eyes widen, face pale. 'It shouldn't be able to do that!'

The furnace spits out flame almost the length of the room, filling it with a wall of fire. 'It definitely shouldn't be able to that either!' He shrinks back against the door, shielding his face.

I try to pull him up. 'Come on, we can't stop!' The furnace responds by belching more fire, faster and hotter, the heat drying my skin. The wall is growing closer.

'How are you going to get past that? She was right, you really are insane!' I wince at the past tense use for Julie. No time to mourn, though.

There's another roar from the furnace but it's muffled. I look to find the darkness covering the furnace, taking its fire. I'm right, the King wants our help. 'It's our chance, Dan!'

I try to pull him along but he ragdolls to the floor with a sob. 'I can't.'

My heart breaks to hear it but I don't have time to argue; the darkness is starting to recede. A creosote smell fills the room—I can't tell if it's from the darkness or the furnace. I run as fast as I can past the furnace. I almost reach the door when the wind, hurricane-strength now, hits me dead in the chest, stealing my breath and pushing me back towards the furnace fire. The darkness is fighting and losing, the fire is slowly getting through. I can feel the heat on my back, my shirt charring. I don't know what to do. I look for any clue from the Crowned King but he's focused on fighting the fire. I gamble and drop to the floor and crawl, the wind unable to hit me as hard though it throws dust in my eyes, blinding me. Voices are shrieking and pleading, 'Stop, you can't!'

I toss a hand on the door and, feeling my way, find the handle. It's being pushed from the other side. The wind again. I shove hard and get nowhere. I try again and this time tumble through the door. It slams behind me. I breathe for what feels like the first time.

I rub my eyes and look around. It's another lab, clear-cased refrigerators with shelves all around. Something cool slides beneath me and I scuttle away, seeing that it's the Crowned King. He stands before me, fully formed. He points to a case that has a single cup in it.

I look at him. 'You want me to get you that cup?' He nods vigorously. 'That's it?' Another nod. I'm disappointed, having expected something grander. I stand, bracing myself for more wind, but it doesn't come. The Crowned King hops up and down, clapping his hands in delight. I swear I can see a smile on his face, though it's only flat darkness.

I yank the plastic door open, breaking some tape as I do. The cup is cold in my hand. It's marked but the ink has faded so it's unreadable. There's more tape sealing it. I offer it to the King but he shakes his head. He mimes opening it. I shrug and do as he requests. Inside is a clear liquid. He gestures for me to give it to him, which I do. He dances once it's in his hand, fist punching the air in victory. The wind kicks up and howls from all directions as its voices shout, 'WHAT HAVE YOU DONE?!'

The King is unmoved and waves it away dismissively, the wind ceasing immediately. The room quiet again, he opens a door I hadn't noticed. It's pitch black outside but a welcome sight. I didn't realize we'd been in here that long.

'What about my friends?' He nods his head. 'You'll help them?' Another nod. That cool whisper in the back of my head speaks, 'I'll take care of them.' I hesitate but he ushers me through. Before I step outside he taps me on the shoulder. I turn around and the contents of the cup are thrown in my face, viscous liquid all over me. I sputter and choke as he pushes me through the door, waving. I land flat on my back, the wind knocked out of me.

I awake impossibly on a busy city sidewalk, coughing and hacking as I stand. People rush by, bumping into me. I cough still and I see him, the Crowned King, a few feet away. He starts parading around and I see crowns now adorning the people he touches, faint but there. It's the last thing I see before I black out.

This time I wake with a cruel cough that hurts my entire body. I can't get enough air. It's a hospital room with lots of curtains and warning signs posted that I can't read. Someone covered head to toe in protective gear is standing beside my bed. 'Congrats,' she says coldly, 'you're patient zero in the newest Corona pandemic.' She doesn't wait for a response and leaves. Where she stood is the Crowned King. He smiles and takes off his crown, gently placing it on my head.

I am the new Crowned King.

cameras and warning signs so small that I can't read. Someone covered head to toe in protective gear is standing beside my bed. 'Corona,' she says coldly. 'You're patient one in the news. Corona pandemic.' She doesn't wait for a response and leaves when she sees the worried look [illegible] smiles and walks [illegible] crowd [illegible] [illegible] head.

I am the [illegible].

ABOUT THE AUTHORS

Josh Schlossberg

Josh Schlossberg is a biological horror fiction author hiding out from past, present, and future pandemics in the foothills of the Rocky Mountains.

He's the creator of Josh's Worst Nightmare (JoshsWorstNightmare.com), founding member of Denver Horror Collective (DenverHorror.com), and managing editor of the best-selling, Colorado-based horror fiction anthology, *Terror at 5280*.

Christy Mann

Christy Mann is an 11 times self-published author and the owner of Twisted Souls Press and Save Your Sanity Publishing Assistance

Writing horror is what keeps her friendly and sane.

www.christymannauthor.com
www.christymannauthor.com/tsp
www.christymannauthor.com/save-your-sanity-publishing-assistance

Archie Kregear

Archie Kregear grew up in Colorado, worked for thirty years in Silicon Valley, and retired to the Kitsap Peninsula in 2018. He is the author of *Mountain Gods*, a novel about what makes people extraordinary, as seen through the life saga of a woman in North Korea. In his writings he strives to intertwine real and fictional science, with believable characters. He enjoys photography and traveling to foreign countries.

Find his book, and others from the Kitsap Writers Group, at kitsapwriters.com. The Researcher is his first published short story.

The author is active on FB, twitter and email at archiekregear@gmail.com.

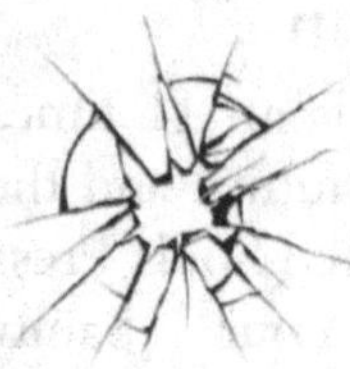

Nick Carlson

My name is Nick Carlson; I am a 22-year-old writer and videographer currently residing in Tallahassee, FL. I've been writing all my life but only fairly recently took the plunge into horror. I self-published my first novel in February, a sci-fi horror about Soviet genetic experiments.

www.nickcarlsonpress.com

www.facebook.com/nickcarlsonpress

www.twitter.com/CarlsonPress

www.reddit.com/user/Nick_Carlson_Press

Ian Neligh

Ian Neligh is an award-winning journalist and author who lives in a rather ominous forest in Colorado.

Juan Ozuna

My name is Juan Ozuna. I live in Phoenix, AZ. I have no publishing credits as of yet, but can read some of my shorter-short stories on reddit under the username, WanderingThrees. I love anything horror, and that is the genre I mainly write.
www.facebook.com/juan.ozuna.100

Solomon Forse

Solomon Forse resides in Silt, Colorado, where he teaches English and writes fiction. If he isn't reading, watching, or writing horror, you'll find him role-playing horror with tabletop RPGs like Call of Cthulhu—or shredding horror on the guitar in his Lovecraft-themed black metal band Crafteon. Follow him on Twitter @SolomonForse or contact him via email at s.forse.writer@gmail.com.
www.witter.com/solomonforse

Sabrina RG Raven

Sabrina RG Raven has over 10 years' experience in the independent publishing field, as an artist, writer, editor and book designer.

Her art and writing styles vary from fantasy and sci-fi to portraiture and book covers. Her first two novels co-written with Mitchell Tierney make up two thirds of the *Everdark Realms* series. Her first solo novel *Blank* is now available.
www.sabrinargraven.com.

Mitchell Tierney

Coming from Queensland, Australia, Mitchell Tierney has written and co-written 6 books. His books range from young adult fantasy and horror to adult horror. He currently has a YA fantasy book titled *The Wandmakers Apprentice* out recently and is in the middle of writing the follow up, as well as his second adult horror novel *The Last of the Woodcutters.*

He can be found at pop-culture conventions a few times a year in Australia and more often than not, at bookstores.

G. Emerald

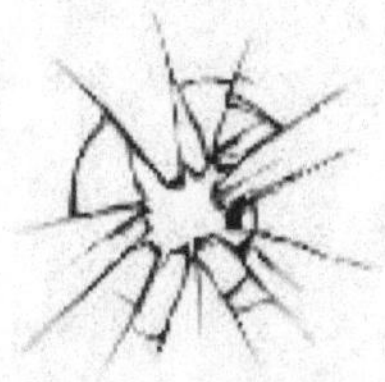

G. Emerald is a new author hailing from rural New York but currently living in Denver, Colorado. She lives with her cockatiel who does his best to help and hinder her writing. She is an avid fan of science and has worked most of her life in medicine. She is also a runner and bird-watcher. Her favorite genre is horror and inhales all things scary. You can find her on facebook as @g.emerald.author.

Social links: @G.Emerald.author at facebook

G. Emerald

G. Emerald is a new author hailing from [illegible] currently living in Denver, Colorado. She lives with her [illegible] She is also a mother and [illegible] You can find her on [illegible]

Social links: @G.Emerald author [illegible]

Twisted Souls Press was founded in 2019 and really started taking shape in January of 2020. With an amazing team, hell bent on producing the best quality dark fiction by some truly amazing authors, publishing horror is our specialty.

We take submissions for themed anthologies twice a year. One is a charity anthology and one is not. We take general submissions for dark fiction quarterly in January, April, July, and October. Check out our website www.christymannauthor.com/tsp for details. You can also follow us on Facebook @TwistedSoulsPress.

The Life On Your Terms Project was founded in January of 2019. The work to get it going as an official 401 (c) is underway but helping people get the things that they need to live life on their terms comes first.

We are always accepting donations and looking for sponsors to increase the number of people we are able to assist and build programs that teach self-sufficiency through entrepreneurship, as well as looking for individuals in need of assistance while transitioning from employment to business ownership.

You can find more information on our Facebook page @tloytp or find more information on our Patreon page. www.patreon.com/christymannauthor

Twisted Souls Press was founded in 2017 and really started taking shape in January of 2018. With an amazing team dedicated to producing the best quality dark fiction by some truly amazing authors, publishing terror is our specialty.

We take submissions for themed anthologies twice a year for charity anthologies and one for us. We take general submissions for dark fiction quarterly in January, April, July, and October. Check out our site www.christymarieauthor.com/tsp for details. You can also follow us on Facebook @TwistedSoulsPr.

The Lift On Your Terms Project was founded in January of 2019. The work to begin becoming an official 501(c)3 is underway, but helping people get the things that they need to live life on their own terms continues. We are always accepting donations and looking for sponsors to increase the number of people we are able to assist and build programs that teach self-sufficiency through entrepreneurship as well as low-income individuals in need of assistance while transitioning from employment to business ownership.

You can find more information on our Facebook page @ or find more information on our Patreon page. www.patreon.com/christymarieauthor